# If I'd Known

*Also by Rebecca Donovan*

## The Breathing Series
*Reason to Breathe*
*Barely Breathing*
*Out of Breath*

## What If

THE *Cursed* SERIES - PART I

# REBECCA DONOVAN

Copyright © 2017 by Rebecca Donovan
All rights reserved.

Visit my website at rebeccadonovan.com
Cover Designer: Ellie McLove
Proofreader and Interior Designer: Jovana Shirley, Unforeseen Editing, www.unforeseenediting.com

No part of this book may be reproduced or transmitted in any form or by any means, electronic or mechanical, including photocopying, recording, or by any information storage and retrieval system without the written permission of the author, except for the use of brief quotations in a book review.

This book is a work of fiction. Names, characters, places, and incidents either are products of the author's imagination or are used fictitiously. Any resemblance to actual persons, living or dead, events, or locales is entirely coincidental.

ISBN-13: 978-0-9995349-1-5

*Dedicated to the Believers*
*~Your heart always knows the truth.~*

# Prologue

We're all cursed—every single one of us.

It's not the compulsions or addictions that will take us down. It's not greed and lust that will bring us to our knees. Our curses are instilled in us as virtues, something we should attain and strive to become. Except it's these traits, the ones we deem to be the most honorable, that cause the most destruction.

I should know. I've been a witness to it my entire life. *Belief, Trust, Kindness* and *Boldness*. They sound like the best characteristics to possess. Except they're the reason for just about everything that's ever gone wrong.

My mother is lost to the *Belief* that love will find her. She still awaits the return of the man who, at the age of seventeen, vowed to always love her.

My grandmother was disappointed each time the *Trust* she had given was betrayed, causing her to be constantly wary of others' motives and intentions.

My aunt Allison allows the wrong people into her life—unable to understand that her *Kindness* doesn't mean others will be kind in return. Three kids with three different fathers later, she lives alone in South Carolina, pregnant with her fourth.

And the eldest, my aunt Helen, cannot advance in the world because her *Boldness* offends more than it inspires.

I wonder if I'm the only one who sees it—the weakness within us. I don't know if we're born cursed or if it's bestowed upon us at some pivotal moment in our lives, but it defines us and ultimately leads to our demise. So we can either accept it or live in denial.

Most live in denial, holding out hope for their "happily ever after."

Well, I hate to say it, but "happily ever after" is bullshit—an illusion concocted to sell books and movie tickets. Yet people want—no, they *need* to believe it exists. They prefer the lies.

Me? I'd rather know the truth, no matter how brutal.

Which is my curse right there ... *Honesty*. I can't remember ever telling a lie, even when I was little. My grandmother was intolerant of anything other than the truth, and so that's all I ever spoke. And why would I want to lie? It's exhausting and takes way too much effort to keep the lies straight.

Every day, I see what lying can do. The false hope. Believing in something that was never real to begin with. Convinced of what will never be.

My curse has taught me how to decipher the bullshit. But telling the truth doesn't always work out so well.

Most of the time, I don't care who I offend. I'll say whatever's on my mind. Ask a question, and I'll give you an honest answer. If you don't really want to know, don't ask.

"Do these jeans make me look fat?"

*Yes. But you are fat, so the jeans have nothing to do with it.*

"Do you think he likes me?"

*No. The fact that he had his tongue down another girl's throat last night should have been a clue.*

"Can we still be friends?"

*No. We were never friends to begin with. You annoy the hell out of me. And I'm totally okay if we never see each other again. Now go away.*

I've come to accept that, regardless of how honest or silent I am, the truth is fated to destroy my life.

# Chapter One

*"Everyone lies, especially boys. You need to keep this"—my grand-mother places her wrinkled finger on my small chest and thumps against my heart—"guarded like a fortress. Don't be fooled by sweet words and a handsome smile, no matter what he promises you. If it sounds too good to be true, it is."*

"I hate you. I really, really hate you," I tell the dirty clothes I shove into the Army bag.

I was supposed to go to the Laundromat last night, but I was too exhausted after my shift and chose sleep. I convinced myself as I collapsed in bed around midnight that I'd get up early and go before school—which was stupid because I'm *not* a morning person. So now, I'm exhausted *and* miserable.

I tuck the small pouch of quarters in the side pocket and set some textbooks on top before pulling the drawstring tight. Dragging the huge tube of clothes behind me, I lock my bedroom door with a click of the padlock and abandon the bag by the front door.

A dark suit is draped over the kitchen chair with a note.

> *Lana, would you be able to drop this off at the dry cleaners for me? If you can't, it's okay.*
>
> *—Nick*

I toss the note onto the kitchen table and pick up the suit jacket. The weight of it and the silken threads *feel* expensive. I hold it in front of me, exposing the satin lining. It has to be tailor-made. I can't even imagine how much he paid for it.

I tell the suit, "You're lucky I like you," but, of course, I mean the man.

Nick met my mother when she was temping as a receptionist at a law firm in Boston about a year ago, but I didn't meet him 'til six months later. He's not the first guy in a suit to be tempted by her fair skin, long blond hair and youthful curves, but he's one of the few worthy of her. Nick's from New York, but he travels between there and Boston regularly. When he's here, he chooses to stay with us, despite the hour and a half commute. He wants to get a place together closer to the city. I think the only reason my mother hasn't given him an answer is because of me.

I've learned not to get involved in my mother's social life. We don't exactly have the same optimistic outlook on love. But it's obvious that Nick is dedicated to taking care of her. And I won't get in the way of my mother's happiness. She deserves to be happy. She deserves him.

I toss the jacket back on the chair. And, just as I begin to walk to the fridge, a clang reverberates against the floorboards. I stop and slowly turn, my stomach already reacting before I see what fell from his suit pocket.

I stare at it for a moment, wishing I'd hated him just like the rest of them.

Now I do.

"Oh, you asshole," I say, bending to pick it up.

Nick's exotic spicy scent enters the room. My jaw clenches as I stand, keeping my back to him.

"Good morning," he says cheerily. "You're up early."

I turn to face him. He must have just taken a shower because his dark hair is still wet, combed neatly and slicked away from his face. Everything about him is expensive—from the crisp white shirt to his perfect, charming smile. He looks so out of place in this dilapidated kitchen. He rolls a suitcase next to him, resting it near the doorway.

I don't respond, only stare, wondering how I didn't see it. I have a gift for knowing when someone isn't who they appear to be—for seeing through the lies. But I never saw this coming. He was so convincing. I *believed* him!

The betrayal burns deep, or maybe it's just my pride that's singed. Regardless, now I want to punch him in the throat.

"Everything okay?" Nick asks, his brows furrowed in concern. "If it's about the suit, I can take it with me, ask the hotel to send it out. I just thought—"

"Or you could ask your wife," I say, cutting him off. I raise my middle finger to reveal the dark titanium band embedded with black diamonds. "Isn't she waiting for you in New York?"

"What ... Lana, I—" he stutters.

"Don't." I shut him up before he can lie again. My voice is edged with venom. "Leave. Never come back. If you do, I'll murder you in your sleep. Understand?"

He remains frozen within the doorframe. His eyes flicker in panic. "It's not ... "

"Piece of shit." I shove past him, causing him to stumble back a step.

I walk to the front door and hoist the straps of the Army bag over my shoulders with a grunt. Without looking back, I warn him, "Tell her the truth, or I will."

"Lana?" My mother's voice carries from her bedroom just before I slam the front door.

I look down at the wedding band on my finger, and my jaw flexes with unrelenting anger. This is going to kill her. Releasing a heavy breath, I trudge down the flight of stairs, the Army bag banging against my thighs with each step. It's practically as big as I am, and I fight not to fall face-first down the stairs.

The street is uncharacteristically quiet when I step outside, only because of the insane hour. The sun's rays peek between the neighborhood buildings, barely having risen itself. The cool morning air soothes my heated cheeks as I walk down the sidewalk.

We don't live in the best neighborhood, but there really isn't a *good* neighborhood in Sherling. At least we don't have gangs tagging every surface. Our street is a small side street, lined with about a dozen multifamily homes. Laundry hangs over porch railings. Broken-down cars take up space in pocked driveways. Most of the time, the sound of arguing or crying kids filters out the open windows, floating along the streets like white noise. I don't really hear it unless it's an overly dramatic fight. So now, with the street vacant of cars and everyone still asleep, the silence makes the anger in my head so much louder.

My mother doesn't belong here any more than he does. I know she's lived here most of her life, but she never quite fit in. She's a dreamer. A believer. A fragile bloom fighting for light in the middle of a landfill. He promised to take her away from all of this. He was supposed to save her from a life that continues to drain the color from her every day.

She sees the good in every person, regardless of who they are or what they've done in life. I always considered this naive. But she genuinely wants to believe every person is worthy. The liars. The cheats. The manipulators. The bastards who use her for their own self-serving needs. Not just the men, but the women too. Those who pretend to be a friend, until jealousy unveils their selfishness and insecurity. They're all the same. But she refuses to give up on them because, when my mother loves, she loves with everything. It's why *Belief* is her curse. It's that belief that will eventually break her.

My fingers curl into a fist, short nails digging into my palm. Oh, I hate him. Everything about him is a lie. I wish I'd seen through him. But he was so sincere. Maybe that's his curse and the reason I couldn't recognize his deception ... *Sincerity*.

If Nick's curse is *Sincerity*, then he's the worst kind of human. Convincing people to believe him, to trust him, only to destroy them when they let him in.

The twenty-four-hour Laundromat at the end of the block is just as deserted as the street, except for the homeless man sleeping under the dryer vent in the alley.

After loading the washer, I sit on the chipped laminate counter and prop my best friend's textbook open on my crossed legs, trying to distract myself from the boiling rage that continues to churn in my stomach.

The distinct ting of a glass bottle rolling along the pavement draws my attention from Tori's algebra assignment. A woman in a leopard print skirt and black bustier stumbles across the street, running a hand through her disheveled dark hair. Smeared liner shadows her eyes, and her lips are smudged with faded red lipstick. I watch her zigzag across the desolate street. She falters when her stiletto heel catches the curb. I wince, expecting her to fall, but she corrects herself with a few stuttering steps.

I try to imagine what she looked like when the night began, confident and sexy. At some point in the night, her curse got the better of her, and this blur of a woman is all who's left.

I finish my English lit assignment just as the dryer rolls to a stop. After placing the folded clothes inside the Army bag, I start back to the house. The neighborhood has slowly begun to stretch its arms during the hour or so I was hidden in the Laundromat. Cars roll up to the intersections, waiting at the lights. Several women in need of their morning coffee stand at the bus stop, tote bags over their shoulders. Voices and music escape out of open windows as I walk past. Peaceful silence has lifted its veil, allowing chaos to resume its reign.

"I don't understand!" Her desperate wails reach me before I can see her. "Why didn't you tell me?"

I stop in front of the neighbor's house to find my distraught mother standing in the middle of our lawn and Nick next to his car with his suitcase in hand.

"I'm so sorry, Faye." His voice cracks in response. "I really am." He turns his back to her and tosses his suitcase in the passenger side of the shiny black BMW.

My mother collapses to her knees when he enters the driver's side without looking back. She covers her face to capture her tears. I can feel her heart breaking from here.

The tires spit out rocks as he tears out of the driveway, leaving a cloud of dust in his wake. Rubber connects with asphalt, and the squeal echoes down the street. I make eye contact with his green eyes and flash him my middle finger, still adorned with his wedding band, meaning every word the gesture signifies. He flinches.

"Asshole," I mutter, wishing I could hang him by his balls.

I turn back to the devastation he left behind—and I don't mean the driveway.

With a heavy sigh, I adjust the straps on my shoulders and approach the frail woman collapsed on the front lawn.

"What are you staring at?" I snap at our neighbor who's standing on her front porch with a coffee mug in her hand, fixated on the spectacle like she's watching a reality show.

She's wrapped in a torn terry robe, her hair a misshapen mass of curls, like she just crawled out of bed—which she probably has. Then again, I know she always looks like this, no matter what time of day. There's no reason to make an effort when she just has to sit at home to collect a paycheck.

"You really shouldn't be allowed out of your house looking like that, Gayle. You'll give the kids nightmares."

A couple of boys laugh as they pass by on their way to the bus stop. The middle-aged woman scowls at me. She glances at the broken heap on the front lawn with a judgmental shake of her head before disappearing inside. The screen door squeaks loudly before it crashes shut behind her.

I can sense others watching too, eyes peering out behind curtains.

I set the bag of clean clothes on the stoop and kneel down beside my mother, my hand on her back. "C'mon, Mom. Let's go inside."

"He ... lied to me," she forces out between broken sobs. She lifts her head from her hands, her big blue eyes bloodshot. "Why ... didn't ... he tell me ... he's still married?"

"Because he's a selfish prick," I tell her, filtering the honesty. If I were truly being honest with her, I would've used a lot more expletives. I wrap my arm around her thin waist and coax her up. "Let's get you inside, so the neighbors don't make money off you on YouTube."

She's not listening to me, but she lets me guide her to her feet. "Why? I don't ... understand. I thought ... he ... loved me. I ... believed him."

"I know you did," I soothe as we slowly move toward the front door. *I did too*, I finish in my head.

I bend down and pull on a strap of the duffel bag, slinging it over my shoulder. I keep one hand on my mother to keep her from toppling into the pit of despair and guide her up the stairs.

We somehow manage to climb to the second floor where the door was left ajar. I shut the marred door with the long, jagged crack down its center and secure the dead bolt.

"Why didn't I know? I should have known," my mother says in hiccuping gasps.

I don't have an answer for her because *I* should have known—which only lights up the fiery rage inside my chest.

"I'm so sorry, Lana," she whimpers, her slender shoulders rounding.

She disappears into her room, and I follow.

"You have nothing to apologize for, Mom," I say with a disheartened sigh.

She slowly sits on the edge of her bed, her shimmery eyes focused on the floor. "I loved him," she whispers, a tear glistening on her flushed cheek.

"I know."

Men with expensive suits and charming smiles have always asked her out when she temps. Understandably. My mother's beautiful and kind—and therefore viewed as an easy target. To them, she's a fling. A disposable hot piece to occupy their time until it hints at becoming serious. Then, they leave. It was a painful lesson. She was forced to learn to be careful with her heart and not fall for every jackass who winks at her.

I'm not the easiest person to get along with. I had to promise I'd back off after threatening too many boyfriends with missing body parts if they hurt her. Let her be the "adult" and make her own decisions. So I refused to acknowledge any of my mother's boyfriends again.

Then came Nick.

Nick was careful with her from the beginning. Asked her out for coffee for their first date and then lunch. Eventually, dinner and a movie. He slowly got close to her. And, in that time, I let him in too.

He was different. Until he wasn't.

I pull back the covers for her to climb in.

It's the same full bed she's slept in since she was a girl. This room is basically the same as when she shared it with her sisters, growing up. Dried flowers hanging from pins along the windowsill memorialize loves lost. Layers of time wallpaper every surface. Photos, art projects, yellowing band posters—constant reminders of the life we'll never escape. It's so … depressing.

Nick's soothing cologne lingers, at odds with the offensive herbal incense my mother burns—another indication that his presence was always a contradiction to everything within these walls.

"Lana, I'm—"

"Sorry. I know." Crimson stains blossom on the white pillow as blood begins to drip from her nose. "Shit, Mom."

I reach for the box of tissues and pull out a few. She takes them from me and presses the cluster under her nose. The hint of dark circles creeps beneath her eyes.

I fumble with the top of the prescription bottle. Dumping a small pill into my palm, I hand it to her along with the glass of water by her bedside. She takes it, swallowing it down.

"I'll get some ice."

By the time I return with ice wrapped in a kitchen towel, a scarlet pile of tissues has overtaken her nightstand. Blood trickles from beneath the tissue, staining her upper lip. I swap out the tissues for a damp facecloth and hand her the ice to apply to the bridge of her nose.

"You're going to be late for school," she mutters in a nasally voice, unable to open her eyes.

"I know." I was always going to be late, but she doesn't need to know that. There was no way I could have gotten the laundry done and still been on time. So now, I'll just be … later. "Will you be okay while I get ready?"

"Go," she urges quietly.

Hesitating a second, I leave the door cracked, so I can hear her if she calls for me.

When I return to check on her, she's asleep. But I know it's a troubled sleep by the way her brows pinch together, the pain apparent behind her lids. I brush the wisps of honey-blond hair away from her face. She's warm to the touch, a hint of a fever. She's been suffering from migraines for as long as I can remember, triggered by stress and ... heartache. I don't know why her body betrays her every time someone else does. Maybe her heart can't handle being broken.

Over the past few months, despite being truly happy, the migraines have kept coming, accompanied by nosebleeds. Last week, she scared us when she grabbed hold of the counter to stay upright. Nick set up an appointment with her doctor for next week, even though she insisted it was nothing.

I watch her for a moment longer. Her face is pale, except for the fully formed shadows under her eyes and the flush of fever on her cheeks. Her lids twitch. This isn't nothing, and it's starting to freak me out.

I refill the glass of water at her bedside and leave a note, telling her I'll call her during lunch and that she has to pick up or else I'll come home. I leave her in her restless sleep as I slip out the front door.

My chest hurts and my whole body is weak with exhaustion. And I wasn't even the one who loved him.

## Chapter Two

*"He didn't love you!" I hear my grandmother yell.*

*I slowly crack my door, just enough so I can see without being caught.*

*"He did! And maybe he still does," my mother cries back, her face wet with tears. "Just let me call him."*

*My grandmother is holding my mom's phone. "If he loved you, then where is he?"*

*My mother's wide eyes are too stunned for words. A cry escapes her mouth as she runs out, slamming the front door behind her so hard, it cracks.*

I hand the forged note, claiming I was at a doctor's appointment this morning, to Mrs. Kellerman in the front office. She gives it a suspicious glance as she scribbles on the tardy slip.

I'm about to walk out the office door when I hear, "Lana."

Maybe if I ignore him, he'll go away.

"I was just going to call you to my office."

I slowly turn, armed with an overly fake smile. "Mr. Garner. You know how much our visits mean to me, but I've had a really rough morning, and I need to get to geometry." It's not easy, being sarcastic and honest at the same time, but I've somehow mastered it.

My smile drops when I see Ms. Lewis in the doorway of his office, her hands on her hips. There's no need to fake anything with her. I can't stand her and she knows it … because I told her in front of the entire class last year when I had her for algebra.

"Sorry, this can't wait," Mr. Garner says, the apology sincere in his eyes. "Hopefully, it won't take long."

With my teeth clenched behind a stiff smile, I give in and walk into his office. I really don't need this. And I'm not exactly in the mood to hold anything back.

"Have a seat." Mr. Garner gestures to one of the thinly padded wooden chairs in front of his desk, closing the door behind me.

I drop my messenger bag on the floor and slouch in the chair with my arms crossed—all contrived pleasantries lost.

He walks around the desk and sits. "You're welcome to have a seat as well, Ms. Lewis."

She chooses to remain standing, sidling next to his desk with her hands still attached to her hips. Her face is pinched in a severe scowl. She's trying to look authoritative. Instead, she looks like she's eaten too many Toxic Waste candies. I ignore her and look to Mr. Garner for an explanation.

"Ms. Lewis is concerned that you may have helped Tori on her algebra test." The silent apology doesn't leave his eyes. He doesn't want to be here any more than I do.

"I'm not in Ms. Lewis's algebra class this year," I answer simply.

The veins protrude along Ms. Lewis's neck, sticking out like chicken bones. She purses her lips even more, struggling to keep from exploding.

"I know that," Mr. Garner says calmly. "I brought that up too. But Ms. Lewis is convinced that you—"

"Cheated!" Ms. Lewis snaps, unable to hold it in any longer. "You cheated! And I won't stand for it!"

"I'm not in your class, Ms. Lewis," I repeat calmly, like I'm talking to a child throwing a temper tantrum. "And didn't Tori take the test in front of you? You were in the room, right?"

Her face reddens and her eyes twitch. It's hard to watch this woman coming apart. I raise an eyebrow in disapproval.

"She is not an A student. It's not possible she did that well on her own!"

"So you're saying you're not an effective teacher? You'd rather believe your students cheated than passed your class?" I question coolly. "Do you get off on flunking your students, Ms. Lewis?"

Ms. Lewis's mouth opens as she blinks repeatedly, a small squeak escaping.

"Lana," Mr. Garner warns. "Ms. Lewis, I know how hard you've worked to get Tori engaged in her classwork. Perhaps your commitment has finally paid off."

Ms. Lewis remains aghast. I think she's about to cry when she storms out of the office.

"I'm glad we cleared that up," I say cheerily, reaching for the strap of my bag as I stand. "Keep doing your thing, Mr. Garner."

"Lana," he calls to me before I can escape.

I slowly pivot to face him. He's wearing a ridiculous lime-green sweater-vest over a blue shirt with a yellow tie. He reminds me of an Easter egg. The man has no sense of fashion. When I look up at him, he's trying to hide an amused smile.

He adjusts the glasses on his face. "I'd really like to make it through the last three weeks of school without adding another page to your file." He rests his hand on top of the three-inch tattered file folder bound with a thick green elastic band.

"I will try to stay away, Mr. Garner. But they keep sending me back to you." I look around the small office, its walls covered with framed cliché posters of achievement and goals. "How can you sit in here all day and not want to break something?"

He lets out a breathy laugh.

Mr. Garner took over for Mrs. Colstrom after she had a heart attack at the beginning of the year. Not my fault, I swear! She was a naive, bubbly little thing who thought everyone could be saved by an inspirational slogan and a lollipop. Unfortunately, there weren't enough lollipops in the world to save me. Instead of wasting her breath on words of inspiration every time I was sent to the office, she'd let me work on my assignments in the library. I actually got more done there than if I'd stayed in class. And, sometimes, I even got to catch up on sleep.

In the short time Mr. Garner's been here, we've become well acquainted, considering I'm sent to his office at least once a week. I blame the *Honesty* curse and defensive educators. He knows I make decent enough grades. I get my assignments done—eventually. And I don't start fights on school property—mostly.

"Be good, Lana," Mr. Garner calls after me as I pass through the office.

My platform shoes clunk loudly on the linoleum as I continue down the hall in my pleated skirt, thigh-high tights and fitted tank. I pass by the dented and busted green lockers of the sophomore wing and reach mine just as the bell rings. The halls fill with a burst of voices.

"Please tell me you told that pruney bitch to sit and spin." Tori appears beside my open locker, sparkling in a strapless sequined top and skintight capris.

"You knew I was going to wear my platforms, didn't you?" I grin, eyeing her five-inch red pumps.

"I can't let you be taller than me when we walk down the hall," she says with a huff. "Besides, I look killer in these shoes."

"Until you start bitching about your feet hurting," I tease. "And, no, I didn't tell the bitch off. But I did question her dedication as a teacher. That didn't go over very well."

Tori laughs. "If she only knew."

"Not my fault she doesn't know how to hide her password."

I printed out the test in advance and helped Tori complete it. Tori pretended to work on the problems during the exam but passed in the correct one at the end—well, not *completely* correct. We didn't want to be that obvious.

"Speaking of"—I reach into my messenger bag and pull out her assignments—"here you go."

"I don't know why you bother. You know it's not important to me." She takes the books from me anyway.

"I'm not starting junior year without you," I tell her.

My motives for doing Tori's homework and papers are purely selfish. She's the only person I claim as a friend in this school, and I won't lose her because she doesn't give a shit about her future. Most of the students in this school don't have a future worth looking forward to—myself included. But being here is better than working a minimum wage job or dealing on the streets. Might as well show up for the next two years.

"It's not like I'll graduate."

"Shut up." I reply. "You *are* graduating."

I made a promise to her father that he'd see her graduate. She'll be the first in his family to actually hold a diploma, and well … I promised. And breaking a promise is worse than lying, so it's happening even if I have to hack into every teacher's computer and do all of her assignments for the next two years.

"Whatever," she says with a dramatic roll of her eyes. "You're coming over after school, right?"

I pause. Tori's eyes tighten.

"I have to go home first. I didn't bring my clothes for tonight."

Tori still appears suspicious. "We're going out. Friday night is *my* night."

"I know. Relax, okay?"

I close my locker, and we begin walking down the hall. We're not in the same class, but Tori has no problem with being late … ever.

"Nick left, and my mom's taking it pretty hard. I want to check on her before we go out." I stop in front of my classroom. "I'll explain at lunch."

Tori shoots me a death glare. "Sorry your mom's sad, but you're *not* bailing."

Tori does whatever she wants, when she wants, and she doesn't care who she has to shove out of the way to do it. I'm her best friend, and even I know she's a bitch. Admittedly, I'm one too. Obviously, *Consideration* isn't her curse. But, ironically, *Loyalty* is.

Somehow, I survive geometry and American government without shoving a pen through my temple.

"What are you up to tonight?"

I try to ignore the voice coming from beside my locker, but sadly, he's still standing there when I close it.

"Nothing with you," I respond. Then I turn and walk away.

But he's persistently annoying. I don't look at him as I strut purposely down the hall, hoping he'll take the not-so-subtle hint.

"There's a party—"

"Not going," I finish before he can tell me where.

"C'mon, Lana. Don't be like that," he pleads, catching up to me.

I continue walking. I think he disappears into the cafeteria as I pass it. But I'd have to be paying attention to him to know. I enter the darkened chemistry lab and pull a key out of my purse. With a quick glance around the empty room, I unlock the closet door and slip inside.

The small space is filled with rows of bottles neatly alphabetized on shelves. This is the period Mr. Tilman "eats lunch" with Miss Hall in the librarian's office, so I know I won't get caught. They're not eating lunch, trust me. I'd pour one of these chemicals into my eyes before sneaking in on that again. But it was worth the lifetime of psychological trauma so I could copy his key to the supply closet.

I didn't steal Mr. Tilman's key for the chemicals, although I could probably make some serious money selling certain ingredients to the right people. I swiped it so I'd have a place to get away from the bullshit that is high school. It's like my own private office ... that smells like sulfur. There are trade-offs for everything in life.

Sitting at the small desk in the corner, I dig for my phone in my bag. I dial my mother twice before she picks up.

"How are you feeling?" I ask her.

"I'm, uh … okay."

"You're not," I counter. Her hesitation makes the lie obvious. "Any more nosebleeds?"

"No."

"Did you eat anything?"

"Not yet. I've been sleeping," she replies, a sob escaping. "Lana, I'll be fine. I'm just … upset. It's nothing you have to worry about."

"Go back to sleep. I'll see you when I get home."

I rest my head in my hand, rubbing my forehead. I *am* worried. I could sit here and curse Nick for convincing my mother he was in love with her. And I do. But there's something going on other than hurt feelings.

I close my eyes against the roiling heat in my gut. I look down at the ring and pull it off, rolling it between my fingers. There's a date etched on the inside—*October 7, 2000*. He's been married for more than sixteen years. My stomach turns at the betrayal.

I slide the ring onto my thumb where it fits perfectly. Good luck explaining this to your wife, asshole.

I find Tori outside the cafeteria, sitting on the stone wall with some girl. I sit next to Tori, opening the yogurt I picked up on my way.

"Hey, Lana," the girl says. "I was just talking about you. I can't believe you turned Bryce down. I don't think he's ever heard the word *no*."

"Or maybe he chooses not to," Tori adds sharply.

"Who's Bryce?" I ask, completely lost. I insert a spoonful of yogurt into my mouth.

The girls look at each other and then at me.

"Bryce Walker. The captain of ... everything," the girl explains in disbelief. "He asked you to a party tonight, and you totally shut him down."

I shake my head, not following, and continue to eat my yogurt.

Tori laughs. "You're unbelievable," she says with a shake of her head.

"Whatever," I reply dismissively. "Is Nina meeting up with us tonight?"

"She has to work the early shift, so she'll be out by eleven thirty," Tori replies.

"What are we doing? The Basement?"

"You get into The Basement?" the girl interrupts, her mouth hanging open.

"Who are you?" I ask, taking a moment to focus on her.

She's thin and angular with her hair pulled up in a messy bun that I know firsthand takes way more time to get right than it looks. She has this European thing about her with the almond shape of her eyes and the thin slope of her nose. She's pretty in an I'm-starving-myself kind of way.

"Emory. We have English lit together."

I nod like it means something. It doesn't.

"Lana doesn't *participate* in high school," Tori explains.

"But she's in class every day—mostly," Emory says, baffled. "You weren't there this morning."

Tori laughs. "I mean, she doesn't get involved in all the gossip bullshit. She has no idea who anyone is. Status means nothing to her."

"And it matters to you?" I question.

"Not really," Tori replies with a shrug. "But I know what's going on. Who's who. It's … entertaining, like a Latin soap opera—overly dramatic and predictable. But you're completely oblivious."

"Because it doesn't matter," I say simply. "We're here for four years. This shit means nothing in the real world, where we actually have to survive."

"Not to us. But to them"—she nods toward Emory—"it defines them."

"That's pathetic."

Emory's face reddens, and I realize I was a bit too honest. I don't apologize for being too honest, otherwise that's all I'd be doing.

"We haven't been to a high school party since … well, it's been a while," Tori delicately explains to Emory.

"But … you're sophomores?" Emory questions, clueless. "I mean, I've *heard* about you, but I just thought … " She doesn't finish. She must realize that what she heard was closer to the truth than most rumors.

I know we have a reputation. I'm not exactly sure what it is, but it's obvious something's being said.

I stand. All the questions are annoying me. Tori stands with me.

"We've gotta go. Thanks for your help earlier," Tori tells her before we walk away.

"Why were you sitting with her?" I ask. "She's—"

"I know," Tori cuts me off with a sigh before I can find an appropriate—or inappropriate—word for the girl. "She let me copy off her earlier today. We had a pop quiz in biology. So you might have to put up with her for a little while until I can ditch her."

I nod, getting it. "Or I can stay away and let you deal with her. She asks too many questions."

"She's just trying to figure out what's true. There are so many stories going around about us; we're practically fictional."

"It's no one's business what we do when we leave here."

"Right. But that's what makes them talk more."

I roll my eyes. "Why do you even bother listening?"

"Because it's funny. There's one rumor that we're involved with the Russian Mafia."

"The Russian Mafia? Seriously? We're in the middle-of-nowhere Massachusetts. I don't think the Russian Mafia even knows this shit town exists. And neither of us is Russian. *You're* Puerto Rican. That's so dumb."

Tori laughs. "Told you it's funny."

I groan. "People are stupid."

"Stupid people have made us legends in this school. Haven't you noticed how everyone acts when we walk by?" Recognizing the unamused look on my face, she adds, "It's not like I care. But again, it makes me laugh."

Just for a second, I look around and watch them follow us with their eyes, whispering. I notice the sidesteps to clear the way. It's not funny; it's sad.

I stop in front of an open door. "You're staying 'til the end of school, right?"

Tori sighs dramatically. "I guess. If I skip technology again, I'll get detention, and there's no way I'm staying in this building longer than I have to. I'll find you after."

I walk into French class and take my usual seat at the back of the room.

"Want to be my partner again today?"

I glance over at Lincoln, opening my notebook. "Sure."

Lincoln's one of the few people I can stand. He doesn't ask dumb questions and focuses on the classwork. He's smart, and he cares about his grades.

There are a select group of students who are actually *trying* to get out of this town. They're the ones who give this building some semblance of a high school, organizing their after-school clubs, participating in sports and driven to make the Honor Roll.

I don't participate in anything, despite Mr. Garner's persistent efforts. Hell, I barely participate in class. The only reason I even know we have sports teams is because I see the players wearing their jerseys on game days. And I know I can skip out early on the days we have pep rallies.

Lincoln's ambitious. I've seen him wear a couple of different game jerseys. I *think* one is basketball. Or it should be since he's so fricken tall. He always has his assignments done for class. He's even helped me finish mine when I've gotten stuck. And I'm pretty sure he's our class president or vice president or something like that. I have no idea what that means exactly, but there were posters up at the beginning of the school year, asking us to vote for people, and I remember seeing his name. I'm not sure if he won, but I hope he did. He's a nice guy.

Halfway through our conjugation assignment, Lincoln leans forward and whispers, "Do you think I have a chance with Tori?"

"What do you mean?" I ask. That question could easily mean so many things. I'm surprised. I would never have guessed she was his type, because he's definitely not hers.

"There's this party tonight in Oaklawn. I was hoping she'd go with me."

"We have plans," I tell him.

"Oh." He lowers his eyes, uncomfortable.

I sigh, recognizing that I sounded like a bitch. "Ask her. I don't actually know what we're doing. If she says yes, then we'll be there."

Lincoln's eyes light up. "Good. A friend of mine was talking about going too."

"Don't set me up."

"Right. No. I'm not," he fumbles. "I was just saying ... we can all ... hang out."

"Sure." I shrug. "Ask Tori first. I'll do whatever she wants."

I walk into Chemistry. I hate this class. Not only because trying to reconfigure molecules makes me want to scorch my brain with a Bunsen burner, but because it's the last class before freedom. It's the worst kind of torture, which means it feels like the longest class of the day. And, to make today even worse, the persistent douche takes a seat on the stool next to mine.

"Why are you sitting here?" I look around and find Paola two tables back, sitting next to a guy wearing a backward baseball cap.

She shrugs her shoulders in apologetic confusion.

"Thought we could be partners today," he says, leaning in and running a finger along my arm. "You know we're good together."

I scoff. "Excuse me?"

"C'mon, baby," he purrs, a pathetic attempt at sounding sexy. "Your hot little body up against mine—now that's chemistry."

I close my eyes and bite my lip, trying so hard not to laugh. But I can't stop it from bubbling up and bursting out of my mouth.

"What?" he asks, grinning without really knowing why.

"Go away," I tell him.

He appears confused. "What did you say?"

"Get off the stool. Go back to your table. And leave me alone." I glare at him, all humor gone. "I'm serious. Get the fuck away from me."

His eyes tighten like he can't believe I just said that to him. "So you're going to be like that, huh?" He smirks like he knows something I don't. "See ya."

Wearing a cocky grin, he stands from the stool and struts back to his table. Paola sits down next to me just as Mr. Tilman walks in the door, flushed and disheveled. Guess he took a long lunch.

"What do you think about checking out a party in Oaklawn? At least until Nina gets out of work," Tori asks me as I shove books into my messenger bag.

I stop what I'm doing and stare at her in shock. "Lincoln asked you? And you said yes?"

"You knew?"

"He asked if I thought you'd go. But I didn't think you'd say yes." I really didn't.

Tori tends to go for the older, bad-boy types. And there are definitely plenty of those in Sherling. Lincoln doesn't really fit into that mold. He honestly doesn't fit in here at all now that I think about it.

"He's sweet. And *hot*." She offers this like it explains everything.

"You don't do sweet," I remind her.

Tori laughs. "I know. That's what's going to make this so fun."

"Oh no. Are you going to destroy this poor guy?" I ask, suddenly worried for him.

I don't know much about Lincoln, but he doesn't deserve to be one of Tori's clawing posts.

"I'm not like that."

I give her a knowing look.

"All the time," she finishes, trying to look innocent. I laugh just as she informs me, "You're going too."

"He's not interested in me."

"He said something about a friend."

"Don't even," I warn her.

She knows how I feel about being forced to be with a guy because my friend is hooking up with his friend. I'm the worst wing-girl.

"I know. I know. But you'll do this for me, right?" she pleads, batting her thick lashes.

"I guess," I reply reluctantly.

She reveals a wicked smile. "We haven't been to a high school party in a couple years. And never in Oaklawn. No matter what happens, this is going to be a night we'll never forget."

I can't argue with that.

"How are we getting there?" I ask. "Let's not go with Lincoln and his friend. I don't want to be stuck with them if you lose interest or if they want to stay and we don't."

"I'll figure something out. Tony might be able to drive us."

"I doubt your brother will want to drive us all the way to Oaklawn."

"He will if you flirt with him." Tori grins suggestively.

"You're awful," I say with a laugh.

It's obvious her brother has a thing for me. I've thought about it. But he's Tori's *brother*, and when it ends—because it *will* end—I don't want it to be awkward every time I go over to their house. So we just flirt because flirting's innocent—mostly.

"What time are you coming over?"

"I'm not sure. But I shouldn't be long. I just have to pick up a change of clothes and check on my mom. I'll text you when I leave my house."

"Oh shit. I don't have Lincoln's number to let him know. I'm going to go find him. Meet me outside?"

"Sure," I reply, closing my locker.

"And maybe I'll find out more about his *friend*."

"Please don't," I beg.

Tori just smiles before walking away.

I lean against the massive stone banister along the front steps of the school, searching for Tori, as everyone floods out through the doors in a mad rush. A red Jeep Wrangler parked along the curb catches my attention—or I should say, the guy leaning against it, who keeps staring at me, does. He looks just like—

"So he *does* exist," Tori says from beside me.

We watch Lincoln approach the Jeep, and the two guys greet each other with a hand clasp and a pound-on-the-back guy embrace.

"Shit. *He's* Lincoln's friend? Are all the Harrison boys that perfect?" When I don't respond, she says, "Lana? You know who that is, right?"

She knows I do, even if he's only ever been talked about like some sort of mystical being.

"This is definitely going to be an unforgettable night."

"Yes, it is," I reply, unable to look away.

Like he knows we're talking about him, he looks up at us, wearing an enchanting smile. I can't force myself to look away, even though I know I should. I continue to watch as he and Lincoln get into his Jeep. I find myself smiling at him when he looks back over his shoulder one more time before driving away.

## Chapter Three

*"If I can tell you one thing," my aunt Helen says, one of the few times she decides to talk to me, "it's don't think that anyone's ever going to give you anything in this life. If you want it, you have to fight for it, even if that means drawing blood."*

"Mom?" I call out as I shut the door and drop my messenger bag to the floor. There's only silence in return.

"Mom?" I say softly, peeking into her room. I'm struck by the potent fragrance of the incense. My eyes water in protest as it burns my nostrils. There's no getting used to that smell.

I quietly enter her room when she still doesn't respond. I find her curled up on her side under the blankets, asleep. Her face is drained of color, except for the ruddy patches on her cheeks. Without touching her, I know she still has a fever. Placing my hand on her forehead only confirms it. She doesn't stir with my touch, which concerns me more.

"Mom?" I say gently, but she doesn't move.

I pick up the water glass and carry it into the kitchen, filling it with cold water from a pitcher in the fridge. Before I bring it back to her room, I glance at her work schedule posted on the side.

Tori's going to kill me.

"I have to work tonight." I close my eyes, braced for her reaction.

"What the fuck?" She doesn't filter the anger in her voice. "You're covering for *her*, aren't you?"

I ignore the spite in her tone. I don't know what Tori's issue is with my mother, but this isn't the time to get into it.

"I get off at ten. What time did you tell Lincoln we'd meet him?"

"I didn't. Lana, this is bullshit, and you know it."

"She's sick, Tori. There's nothing I can do about it. You know that."

And she does, which is why she doesn't tell me to get someone else to cover for her. We can't afford to miss a shift.

"I'm picking your ass up right at ten o'clock. Be ready."

"I'll need to shower before we go out."

There's silence.

"Tori, I can't smell like the diner. It's disgusting."

After another dramatic moment of silence, she finally says, "Fine. I'll ask Tony to pick you up. But we have to leave my house by ten thirty. Tony's going out, and he's our ride to the party."

"I'll be so quick, I promise," I assure her. It's not like she's giving me any other choice. "I've gotta go. But I'll see you tonight."

I sort through the bag of clean clothes, pulling out my hideous hunter-green polyester uniform. I swear the dress was made out of a leisure suit. It might even be flame retardant. The only good thing about it is that grease, ketchup and beer wash right out of it, and it never needs to be ironed.

Unlike my favorite jeans that got ruined last weekend when Nina threw up on me. If she'd eaten, she might've been able to hold down whatever that bright pink drink was. So gross. Now they will have to become my favorite cutoffs. But I don't have time to mess with cutting them right now.

I opt to pack a pair of fitted white lace-trimmed shorts, a low-cut bright sea-blue halter top and wedge sandals that wrap around my ankles. I drape my cropped black leather jacket over the tote and proceed to dress in the hideousness that is my uniform.

Luckily, my mother has the dinner shift, so I don't have to deal with the *totally* obnoxious drunks. Stella's technically a diner. But, really, it's a bar ... that serves horrible food. The people who frequent Stella's aren't here for the menu. They're here for the cheap beer and strong well drinks. They'll eat anything to sop up the puddle of liquor in their stomachs. The greasier, the better.

I have no idea who *Stella* is. Margo owns the place. Jim runs it. No one ever mentions Stella or why the place is named after her. All that's left of her is a black-and-white photo of a blonde sitting on the back of an old convertible, blowing a kiss at the camera with *Stella* scrawled in smeared blue ink on the white border. She's surrounded by pictures of motorcycles and muscle cars along with a framed dollar bill. Whoever she was, the sentiment is now lost in the chaos.

I've been working here since before it was legal for me to have a job. I started two years ago when my mother was sick for a week and we couldn't afford the lost wages. It's not like this place offers sick days or vacation. One day, I came in and clocked in under her name. No one cared as long as I could balance plates and not spill beers.

"Lana, hook us up with a pitcher?"

I take a moment to actually look at the acne-faced guy who thinks he knows me. I sure as hell don't know him, although I have a feeling we go to the same high school.

"Why should I?" I ask him. "What do you got that I want? And *think* before you answer that because I definitely don't want you." I eye his scrawny frame critically.

The acne victim's mouth drops as his friends start laughing.

"Uh, how about this?" He reaches into a pocket and pulls out a small sealed plastic bag filled with pills of various colors, another smaller bag of white powder and a joint.

"What are you doing, man?" the guy across from him questions sternly.

With a quick warning glance, he continues, "We call it 'party in a bag.'" He smiles like he's clever.

I don't change my bored expression, although I like the sound of it.

I take the bag from his hand before he can react and slip it into my apron pocket. I turn and walk away without a word, returning with a pitcher of beer and a stack of glasses.

I drop their check.

"You charged us for the pitcher?" he asks incredulously. "I thought—"

"Don't," I threaten. "If this is any good, I can hook you up with *partiers*."

He shuts his mouth, knowing I could easily triple his business just by dropping a few words to the right people.

"Hey, sweetness, can we get another round?" a guy calls, his face hidden behind a shrubbery of facial hair.

He raises his hand to swat my ass. I can feel the gesture before I see it. Since I started working here, I've adapted a sixth sense for sexual advances. And these scumbags have tried just about everything.

"Touch my ass, and I'll make sure there's shards of glass in your beer," I warn him.

His hand lowers under the table.

I drop their ticket. "If you're just staying for drinks, you can walk the three feet to the bar to get them yourselves."

"Lana, can you take that table of guys who just sat down?" Marisa asks as I walk by her, dumping plates on the metal counter for the dishwasher.

"That's not my table," I tell her, not about to be nice at nine forty-five. "I'm off soon anyway. Sorry."

I don't stick around to hear her complain. I pick up the plates waiting for me on the raised stainless counter, hiding the shit show that is the kitchen. If people saw what happened back there, they'd never eat here again. I shuffle around the bodies hanging out at the counter … or bar. Whatever it is, it's the worst setup ever.

I drop the plates on the table, not caring if the correct order is in front of the right person. They're my last table.

I need them to eat and settle up, so I can get the hell out of here. Tony should be here soon, and I know Tori won't let me hear the end of it if we don't leave her house by ten thirty.

"Anything else?" I ask, leaving the check without waiting for an answer. "If you need another drink, you can get it at the bar."

Technically, I'm not supposed to serve alcohol. I'm only fifteen. But Jim and Margo ignore the law. And the police are too preoccupied with what happens in the parking lot to notice what happens *inside* this metal Twinkie.

It's a job. I can't afford *not* to be here. And, believe me, I *constantly* remind myself of this too.

I clear my other tables and make sure they've all paid before returning to the table I just fed. "Ready to pay?" I ask.

They're interfering with my night. If they don't like the not-so-friendly service, they came to the wrong place. Besides, I'm not counting on the crappy tip they never planned to leave me.

A guy with tattoos covering his thick arms pulls out two twenties and drops them on top of the bill without looking at it.

"Need change?"

He shakes his head. I try to hide the surprise that flashes across my face with a blink. Maybe he can't count. I'm not about to offer a math lesson. I hand the cash to Margo at the register and wait for the change. All she does is handle the money. She doesn't trust anyone. Not even Georgia or Mal, who've worked the bar since before I was born. No one touches the cash other than Margo, who remains perched on her wooden stool, watching everyone with her beady blue eyes.

She reminds me of a bird, frail and thin, with wrinkled skin hanging off her, scowling at everyone like she's tempted to peck their eyes out. She sees *everything*. I try not to talk to her. I try not to even look at her if I can help it. She creeps me out.

I duck into the back, past the counter where plates of food are waiting to be picked up. "Jim, I'm clocking out."

"No you're not," he bellows. "You have five minutes left in your shift. Go check the bathrooms."

I stop, wishing I had kept my mouth shut and just clocked out. He would never have known.

As soon as I push open the red metal door, I'm forced to cover my mouth and nose. The stench is overwhelming. One of the toilets isn't working. Jim knew and didn't want to deal with it himself. Bastard. Well, I'm definitely not going to unclog it. Women are disgusting. I'm convinced we're grosser than men—throwing who knows what into the toilets, pissing all over the seats, littering the floor with shreds of toilet paper that are destined to stick to the bottom of someone's shoe. There's no way I can get away with leaving it like this. I'll get reamed the next time I work.

I pull on latex gloves and pick up the fragments of paper towels and toilet paper scattered on the floor, shoving them into the overflowing trash. I wipe down the chipped porcelain sinks and step down on the trash to compact it.

Taking the trash bag with me, I walk out the back door to toss it in the dumpster. When I try to go back in, the door's locked. I groan. Of course it is. I'm *never* getting out of here. I'm forced to walk all the way around to the front where there's a line to get in.

A car honks. I turn my head just as Tori pulls herself out the passenger window, sitting on the edge of the door.

"Why are you here? I thought I was coming to your house?" I question, recognizing she's dressed to go out.

"Change of plans. Tony's meeting friends, so we have to go now or else we won't have a ride."

Tony nods with a subtle grin in the driver's seat. I smile back, biting my lip to keep it from being too big.

I look down at my hideous, stained uniform that smells like grease and beer, knowing the rest of me pretty much smells the same. "But I'm repulsive."

"Put on extra perfume. Besides, guys love the smell of this place. You may even get licked tonight," Tori teases wickedly.

I shoot her a disgusted look.

My skin feels like I have a layer of oil clinging to it, and I don't even want to know what my hair is doing.

"Seriously, Tori?" I gripe. With a frustrated sigh, I turn toward the line blocking the front door.

"Hurry up!" Tori hollers in return.

I push my way through the bodies, not bothering to excuse myself. It wouldn't help. This crowd responds better to brute force. And I desperately need to get out of here.

And *now* there's suddenly a line to get into the bathroom. The clogged toilet's probably not helping.

I grit my teeth in frustration. "You've got to be kidding me." This night just keeps getting better and better. Hell, this entire day has been shit. Might as well keep it coming.

I slip into the kitchen without being seen by Jim and past the grill where Carlos is flipping hockey pucks. Some of them, I know, are supposed to be pancakes. I glance at him, and he winks at me.

"Going out tonight, beautiful?"

"Trying," I respond.

Carlos is a flirt but harmless. A guy who feels compelled to compliment Margo's bug eyes is pathetic, not threatening. I seriously doubt he's ever had a girlfriend in his life. I kinda feel sorry for him. Until I catch him staring at my ass and have to fight the urge to punch him.

I clock out at five past ten, grab my bag and try Jim's office door so I can change. It's locked. Why is it impossible to get out of here tonight? I hide myself in the corner the best I can and slip my shorts on under my dress. I unzip the green monster and let it fall to the floor, quickly pulling the halter top over my head and removing my bra beneath it. When I turn around, Carlos is staring with his brows raised and a spatula hanging limp in his hand.

"What?!" I question accusingly, trying not to think about what he might've seen.

He just stares at me dumbly.

I ignore him and pick up my crumpled uniform, shoving it into my bag. I exchange my black sneakers for the strappy wedge sandals. I don't have a mirror, so I use the camera on my phone to check my makeup. Running a finger under my eyes to capture the smears only makes it worse, so I add dark liner and smudge it for a smoky effect and finish with shiny pink gloss on my lips. I gather my hair into a knot on top of my head and slide on a sparkly crystal headband to hold back my bangs. Despite the effort, I still *feel* like a mess. I'm just hoping *hard* I don't look it.

I exit the back door without saying anything to Jim. I clocked out. I'm done.

I spritz perfume on my neck and wrists then spray it in the air to walk through it, desperate to conceal the *eau de Stella's*. As long as I don't act like a mess, no one will know. Right? That's what Tori always tells me.

*"Act the way you want everyone to see you, no matter how you're really feeling."*

I haven't quite mastered it. I tend to be way too expressive. My feelings are always evident all over my face, even when I try to hide them.

"Fake it 'til you make it." Great. Now I'm quoting posters from Mr. Garner's office.

I open the back door of Tony's car and throw my bag across the seat before sliding in. "Okay, bitch, let's go to this fucking party."

## Chapter Four

*"Never let a boy lay a hand on you," my grandmother says sternly, pointing a finger in my face. She looks angry. But I don't remember doing anything wrong. And a boy definitely didn't touch me. "Do you understand me? Not ever."*

*I nod, too scared to ask what she means.*

"House party in Oaklawn, huh?" Tony pulls into the circular driveway lined with cars.

"Hey," Tori declares defensively, "we *never* go to house parties."

"Maybe because no one we know owns a house." I eye the people wearing plaid and jeans, standing outside the house, holding red Solo cups. It's like walking onto the set of a CW show. I had no idea that these kinds of parties really existed.

"You'd never catch me at one of these white-boy parties," Tony says with a chuckle.

"We're not staying. I told Lincoln I'd meet him here; that's all. Nina's picking us up after she gets off work,"

Tori explains, as if she has to keep defending why we're here.

I don't know why she's so sensitive about it. Maybe because she always wants her four older brothers to think she's badass, and this party is anything but.

"Don't call me if you get stuck," Tony tells his sister. "Lana, call me if you need a ride."

His dark eyes find me in the rearview mirror and I wink.

"Asshole," Tori throws at him, getting out of the car. "C'mon, Lana."

I grab my bag and slide out.

"Don't have too much fun without me," Tony says to me, flashing a devilish smile before driving away.

"You two need to get it over with," Tori grumbles, walking toward the open front door of the huge white house.

"He's hot, but I'm *not* hooking up with your brother," I tell her *again*.

"The flirting is making me nauseous."

"Too bad," I say with a laugh. "It's better than hearing me scream his name in the room next to yours."

"Ew," she groans, scrunching her nose in disgust.

"Exactly," I reply, smiling.

"Fine. I get it," Tori snaps, nudging through the packed bodies in search of alcohol—or at least, I hope she is.

Without warning, Tori turns around and faces me. I stop short.

"What?" I try to look over her shoulder, thinking she saw someone she doesn't want to run into.

"Be nice," she instructs, almost threatening.

"You're telling *me* to be nice?" I let out a short laugh at the irony.

"Whatever," she says with an eye roll. "I just mean that I know these aren't exactly our people, but I want to see what Lincoln's all about. He's ... different. And I don't want you ruining it with your *honesty*."

I laugh. "I will *try*," I assure her. "But I make no promises."

She sighs and turns back around, leading us through a huge crowded room, everyone drinking and laughing. We finally emerge into a large open kitchen, but I still don't see any alcohol, only abandoned red cups and half-eaten bowls of chips and pretzels.

"Where do we get a drink?"

I'm suddenly nervous. Maybe we needed to bring our own, even though Tori promised me they'd have plenty here. We never go to parties where the alcohol is free. It always costs something.

Tori scans the crowd until a smile emerges on her face. I follow her gaze and find Lincoln. It's actually hard to miss him since he towers over everyone ... and he's like the only black guy here.

"I need alcohol," I tell her as she starts in his direction.

She doesn't respond. Maybe she didn't hear me, but I can't stay at this party and remain sober. I squeeze through the crowd and spot a keg on the back porch.

"Of course there's a keg," I mumble, feeling stupid for doubting that *this* party wouldn't supply drinks.

The apartment parties we've been to, you have to fend for yourself—bring your own and then guard it for the night, so no one steals your stash. Girls usually flirt— or some loose interpretation of that word—to get drinks, but that also means being stuck with that guy for the rest of the party.

I always make sure we come stocked with our own alcohol. There's no way I'm going to be dependent upon a guy for drinks, and I'm definitely *not* owing him for my buzz.

I tug on my bag and struggle to get through the crowd until I'm finally outside in the open space of the deck, slightly annoyed. I don't usually carry big purses, and getting caught on everyone who walks by is driving me crazy. I need to stash it somewhere. I'm not worried about it being taken. It's not like anyone here is going to care about a beaten-up tote. I'm wearing the leather jacket with my tip money hidden in the inside pocket, and my phone's zipped in the outer one. I pat the other pocket to make sure I put the "party in a bag" in there. I walk down the steps and around the side of the deck, hiding my tote in the darkest corner underneath. If anyone really wants the hideous uniform and shitty sneakers, they can have them.

"What're you doing over here?" I hear as soon as I stand back up. "Are you getting sick?"

"Uh, no," I reply sharply. "What are you doing over here? Looking for a victim?" I walk past the gargantuan dude who stares after me silently.

As I wait in line at the keg, I can *feel* the eyes on me. From everywhere. I scan the crowd and curse Tori under my breath. Of course they're staring—with my ass cheeks peeking out of my lacy shorts and the cleavage revealed within the cowl of the low-cut halter. Where we usually go out, no one would think twice about what I'm wearing. Not here. I'm getting scanned up and down, like they're trying to decide if they should threaten me to stay away from their boyfriends or offer me fifty for twenty minutes in the backseat.

"Who are you, and why are you at my party?"

There's a guy in a blue polo shirt and khaki shorts next to me. He looks like most of the guys here—throw in a baseball hat here or there or a random button-down hanging over a T-shirt.

"I'm here for the free beer," I tell him with a sardonic smile.

He smiles back. "Then let's make that happen. Excuse me, guys," he tells everyone waiting ahead of me in line. "The lady needs a beer."

A moment later, he hands me a filled red Solo cup. "Here you go."

"Thank you." I take it from him and offer a small smile, not enough to encourage him to stick around.

"My name's Blake. Let me know if you need anything, okay?" And, just like that, he's rushing off to help some other girl in need of a shot. "Whitney, I have Fireball for you!"

"Who are you anyway?" a girl asks from behind me. "Who'd you come here with?"

It's not a friendly let-me-introduce-myself question. It's a total territorial you-have-some-nerve-showing-up-here question.

"It's not about who I came here with," I tell her with a smirk. "You should be worried about who I *leave* with."

She gasps in mock horror. I fight the urge to roll my eyes.

I enter the house and find an empty spot in the corner of the kitchen. I don't bother looking for Tori and Lincoln. I'm *not* third-wheeling it. I'm prepared to hang out here, lean against the counter and observe the spectacle happening around me 'til it's time to go.

"Where are you from?"

"Can you believe she even thinks she has a chance with him?"

"You're not from Oaklawn, right? I know I'd remember you."

"And did you see what she's wearing? That diet's definitely *not* working."

"Oh shit!"

Girls scream as a drunken ass collides with them, barely making it in time to throw up in the sink.

I'm a captive audience to the Middle America drama. The gossip. The terrible pop music blaring through the speakers. The amateurs who can't handle what's in their cups. The couple pressed against the wall, making out, his hand up her shirt. And, yes, I'm aware a guy's standing next to me, trying to get me to talk to him.

"What did you say your name was?"

When he refuses to take a hint after I continue to blatantly ignore him, I release an impatient breath and say to his face, "Go away."

He looks offended. I laugh at him.

"Bitch."

"Undeniably," I agree.

He scowls and shoves a path to the living room where a group of girls are failing to make dancing happen.

And then ... I see his bright blue eyes. The same captivating shade as his brother. And, most likely, their father's. The eyes that wouldn't look away when he saw me at school earlier today and that hold me in place now.

He smiles, and a deep dimple creases his right cheek.

"Shit," I breathe out.

He remains focused on me as he navigates the crowd. People talk to him along the way. He responds but doesn't take his eyes off me and never stops moving in my direction. I am pinned to this spot, anticipating his approach until he's finally in front of me. And I mean *right* in front of me. His hand rests on the counter next to my waist as he bends down, and his lips brush my ear.

"Hey, Lana."

A shiver shoots down my spine.

"How do you know me?"

He doesn't pull away. My mouth is so close to his skin, I could easily suck on his neck.

"Who doesn't know you?" he says, his voice a low rumble that sends a jolt through my heart. He leans away to look me in the eye.

I laugh. "Just about everyone here."

"This isn't usually your scene." There's an ease rolling off him, like he's comfortable with the attention. He's definitely getting plenty of that from just about everyone around us—for completely different reasons than I am.

"No, it isn't." I nod toward Tori, who's laughing flirtatiously at something Lincoln said, placing her hand on his arm. "Being a good friend. So you're *the* Joey Harrison? I thought you were a myth."

He laughs, standing to his full height. And I'm regretfully aware of the distance between us.

"Yeah, I don't come home much anymore."

"Where do you hide?" I take a gulp of the chilled beer, needing to cool down.

"I go to a private school up north."

I smirk. "Of course you do."

He narrows his eyes, confused by my response.

"I'm glad you're here." He hasn't glanced around once.

I can't say I'm uncomfortable with his unwavering attention, but it's definitely intense.

"Are you now?" I tease with a grin, trying to appear unaffected.

He flashes a devilish smile before taking a sip of his beer. "Want to get out of here? We were thinking of trying another party."

"Who's 'we'?" I've learned that committing to leaving with a group of guys can lead to complications later.

"Lincoln, me and Vic." He nods to the guy leaning against the counter across from us.

I hadn't noticed him before now. He stands out worse than I do in his leather jacket with his clean-shaven head and a large tattoo scrawled up his neck and etched across his skull. He looks like sunshine walking. By that I mean, depressing as hell.

"I'm not sure what we're doing, but we're leaving as soon as our friend gets here." I scan the kitchen and locate the clock on the microwave. "Which should be soon."

Joey pulls his phone from his pocket, examining the screen. "Excuse me a second?"

"Take all the seconds you need," I tell him, impressed by the request.

He has more manners than most adults I know. But then again, I work at a dive bar.

Joey exits the sliding door onto the deck, his phone to his ear.

I glance over at the scowling mass across from me and try to figure out how that friendship happened. Vic doesn't make eye contact, but I can almost hear him growling. Charming.

"Where's Joey? I saw him talking to you," Tori asks, appearing out of nowhere. "Please don't tell me you pissed him off already."

"I'm not *that* big of a bitch," I reply defensively.

Tori shoots me a look, silently challenging my statement.

I roll my eyes. "He's outside on the phone."

"That must be where Lincoln went," she tells me. "So, do you mind if we hang out with them tonight?"

"Tori, did you meet Vic?" I grin wickedly and nod toward him. "He's with the guys."

Tori turns with a huge smile to greet him, but before she can open her mouth to say anything, she takes him in, and the smile vanishes. "Oh no," she says, eyeing him up and down, openly judging. She turns back to me. "Seriously? Nina is not going to be okay with"—she eyes him and makes a face like he smells foul—"*him*."

I keep wearing my wicked grin, amused by her reaction.

"This is bullshit," she complains loud enough for Vic to hear her.

"When is Nina getting here?"

"I was about to text her," she says, opening her purse and pulling out her phone.

"Hey, ladies," Joey greets us, a beautiful smile spread across his face. "Wanna come to The Point with us? I got on the list."

"You did?" Tori's brows rise. "I thought The Point was exclusive and impossible to get into?"

Joey shrugs with a confident grin. A smile blooms on Tori's face, her eyes lit. Tori knows I've been dying to get into a Point party for forever but haven't been able to get access. She doesn't even have to ask if I want to go; she already knows the answer.

"The only problem is, we need a ride. My brother took my Jeep, and I have to get it from him when we get there."

"Umm ... let me see if I can make that happen," Tori says, lifting her phone to her ear and walking out onto the deck, away from the noise.

"How did you get on the list?" I ask Joey, beyond impressed.

"My brother owes me," he explains vaguely.

"We have a ride!" Tori announces a minute later. "Nina hooked us up. She'll be here in thirty."

I consider for a second who Nina could be getting a ride from. Maybe one of the girls at the club? I hope so because I don't want her to feel like she needs to entertain Doom and Gloom all night.

"Play a round of beer pong with me while we wait?" Joey takes my hand like he's about to lead me away.

"Uh, no," I respond, not moving.

"You've never played before," he accuses with a smirk.

I open my mouth to deny it, bothered by his assumption. But I can't lie. "No."

He pulls me after him, not allowing me to resist. "C'mon. We're doing this."

After filling our keg cups, Joey leads me downstairs to the finished basement where a small crowd surrounds a ping-pong table. There's a couple standing at either end of the table with a cluster of cups spread out in front of them. A girl takes aim with a ping-pong ball before tossing it, landing it in a cup. Everyone chants, "Drink," as the other couple takes gulps from their beers and then removes the cup from the table.

Resting his free hand on my hip, Joey bends down to explain the rules, speaking directly into my ear, the way he did earlier. At the low murmur of his voice, I catch myself inadvertently leaning into him as I listen. When I feel his chest against my back, I stand up straighter, pulling away. I don't let guys touch me, not so intimately anyway. I need to know they're worth my time before I get close. But I keep gravitating toward Joey. His hands feel like they belong on my body. I step away from him, and his hand falls away. With the release of his touch, I'm snapped awake—once again very aware of the vacant space between us.

"Harrison, do you have a partner yet? You play winner," a guy in a pink polo shirt calls to Joey from across the room.

Joey grins and points to me. The pink polo shirt guy smiles wide, like he approves of Joey's choice. I fight back the urge to roll my eyes—oh-so glad I have his approval.

Within a few minutes, one cup remains on the farthest side of the table, and the guy on the opposite end sinks the ball. Everyone hollers and cheers while the losing couple chugs their beers.

"This is a stupid game," I observe out loud.

Joey laughs and takes my hand to lead me to the losers' end.

"Think of it as one of those carnival games," Joey says from behind me so that only I can hear. "You know, the ones where you have to toss a ring around a bottle or throw darts at balloons. Except we need to get a ping-pong ball into a bunch of cups and force people to drink."

"Do I get a prize if we win?" I ask sarcastically, realizing too late that he could easily misinterpret that question.

Joey laughs, revealing the deep dimple with his beautiful smile. "If we win, I'll make sure you go home with a prize," he promises, "even if I have to buy you a stuffed monkey."

I grin, grateful that he didn't turn the comment into an invitation to get in my shorts. "I'd prefer a zebra."

This makes him laugh again.

"Ready?" the guy at the other end calls to us impatiently.

"Let's win me a zebra," I say, earning strange looks from the spectators who heard me.

And we do win. It may have helped that the other team just played three games and were kinda drunk. Or it could have had something to do with the fact that I'm pretty damn good at this stupid game. Not bragging or anything, but I'm impressive, sinking the ping-pong ball in cup after cup, earning cheers and high fives from the onlookers. And a bear squeeze of a hug from Joey when I nailed the winning shot, which made it difficult to breathe for more than one reason. Wow, he's built.

Who knew that the best way to fit in at a party was to kill them at their own game?

"Who's up next?" one of the losers asks. They have names, but I don't remember them.

"We've gotta go." Joey's announcement is met with groans.

That's when I notice the same bitchy girl from earlier glaring at me from across the room. When he takes ahold of my hand, like we're meant to be together, I can't help but smirk at her, which only makes her angrier. So, of course, I laugh.

"What?" Joey asks, looking in their direction. He must catch on before I say anything because he pulls me closer, settling his hand on the small of my back as he guides me away.

I check my phone while we climb the stairs and find a text from Tori from two minutes ago. Nina's out front. Waiting.

"They're out front," I tell Joey, abandoning my empty beer cup next to some expensive-looking sculptures on a table in the hallway.

As soon as we step outside, I remember, "Oh. My bag."

"Where'd you leave it?" Joey asks.

"I'll be right back," I tell him, releasing his grasp to rush along the side of the house. I duck down in the shadows and reach under the deck for my bag.

When I stand, there's someone behind me.

"Got it," I say, assuming it's Joey.

Except this guy's much bigger.

"Knew you'd show up to find me," he says, hovering a little too close.

"You're delusional," I tell him, moving to walk past him.

He grabs my arm, whipping me around to face him. "Where do you think you're going?"

I stare up at the same annoying guy from earlier today at school. The guy who obviously *won't* take no for an answer. I search for his name but can't bring it to the surface. God, I really suck with names.

"Don't touch me." I slip my free hand into my jacket pocket.

"You think you're too good for me?"

"Yes," I say, realizing too late that the answer should've remained in my head. "But don't take it personally. I'm too good for most guys."

That didn't help. His grip on my arm tightens as his cockiness turns bitter.

"You're such a fucking bitch."

"I should really have that tattooed somewhere," I say, removing my hand from my pocket and pressing the button. "Now let go of me or I'm going to tattoo my name on your balls."

He glances down at the blade glistening between his legs.

"Lana?"

I don't redirect my eyes from the douche who's cutting off the circulation in my arm.

I gently tap the crotch of his jeans with the flat part of the blade. He jolts away like I've shocked him. I don't hesitate to escape, finding Joey waiting for me at the front corner of the house. I ease the blade back into the handle and conceal it in my pocket just as I reach him.

Joey eyes me curiously, glancing behind me. "Everything okay?"

I provide the most honest answer I can offer at this second. "I need a drink."

Nina, Tori and Lincoln are standing beside a car I don't recognize. It's huge and old. It looks like a tan tank with a black canvas top. When I look more closely, I notice Gary, Nina's boss from the strip club, in the driver's seat. What the hell? He's the biggest perv in existence. Way too many hands touching girls who are barely legal. I met him once and had to shower immediately after from just being molested by his eyes. Why is he here?

"Finally!" Tori exclaims when she sees us approaching. She grabs my arm and pulls me away from everyone. "Where have you been? You didn't get in a fight or anything, right? I was getting worried when I couldn't find you. I had a bad feeling because half of these girls are skanks, and I was about to claw someone if I had to stay at this party a single second longer, so I knew you were probably on the edge of taking someone out. Is everything okay?"

"Take a breath, Tor." I raise my hands for her to see that they're blood-free.

There's obvious relief in her eyes.

When we turn back to the car, everyone's seated inside, not leaving us many options. Tori glares at Vic, who is sitting in the middle of the backseat, between Joey and Lincoln. I know she wanted to be the one sitting near Lincoln. She opens the passenger door and slides in beside Nina.

I'm about to squeeze in after her when she looks up at me and says, "Sit in the back," followed by a wink.

She closes the door before I can respond.

When I open the back door, Joey is smiling up at me.

"Hey," I say, unable to hide my smile.

He pats his lap. "C'mon in, pretty girl."

## Chapter Five

*"Lying is the worst kind of betrayal."*

*I watch the tear drip from my mother's nose onto the pillow as I lie across from her in bed, her hand holding mine tightly.*

*"Don't ever lie to protect someone from the truth. Untrue words hurt as much as a knife to the heart."*

"Are you comfortable?" Joey asks, leaning in so that his voice hums in my ear.

I'm beginning to think this is his way of unraveling me. It's more intimate than the hand he has resting on my hip. I tilt my head toward him, my cheek brushing against his freshly shaven skin. He smells so good. I almost close my eyes to inhale him.

"I am," I reply, leaning a little farther back into the corner of the car, my legs draped across his, so I have a better view of him.

"I'm impressed with your beer pong skills." His mouth quirks, giving a hint of his dimple. "You sure you haven't played before?"

"I'm sure." I smile wryly. "You owe me a zebra."

"I do."

He's slowly moved closer, so now he only has to lean his gorgeous head in just a little to kiss me. Lost in his attentive gaze and seduced by the low rumble of his voice, I *want* him to kiss me. I brush my hand along his neck, transfixed.

"Want some?"

It's like someone shook me and I'm awakened from a trance, dropped back into the middle of reality with music blaring and bodies squeezed in next to us. I catch Nina's scrutinizing eyes in the rearview mirror. Whatever she sees, she isn't happy about it. I remove my hand from Joey's neck and sit up a little straighter.

Tori leans over with the bottle in her hand. "Lana?"

"Sure," comes out way too wistful. I clear my throat. Not bothering to look at what I'm drinking, I hold my breath and take two long gulps, breathing out against the astringent peppermint burn.

I offer the bottle to Joey. After taking his share, he passes it to Vic.

"Hey," I say when Vic makes eye contact.

"Vic, this is Lana." Joey nods toward me. "Vic and I go to school together in Vermont."

"What's up?" Vic nods with a quick lift of the thick black eyebrows that shadow his sunken grey eyes.

After he takes a long swig from the bottle, he hands it to Lincoln and crosses his arms. The energy rolling off him is dark and brooding. I can tell he's going to be as much fun to have around as the plague. I haven't wanted anything to do with him since I first saw him at the party, and that hasn't changed.

"How you doin', Lana?" Lincoln asks, his long legs bent uncomfortably behind the front seat.

I never know how to respond to that question. People don't really *want* to know the miserable truth. And I can't lie and tell them what they expect to hear, so I offer an ambiguous shrug.

Even though I saw him at the party, this is the first time Lincoln and I have spoken tonight.

"I didn't know you and Joey were friends."

"You and I don't exactly talk about things like that," he replies.

That's true. I've been his partner in French just about all year, and I don't know much about him other than he plays sports and has a scholarship to go … somewhere. Oh, and that he apparently has a thing for Tori.

Most guys do.

Tori isn't exactly girlfriend material. So I wouldn't have encouraged him if I had known he was seriously into her. She's never been exclusive with a guy for as long as I've known her, which is practically forever. She's distant but flirty. Something about her aloofness comes across as untouchable. And predictably, guys want what they can't have, making her that much more alluring. Tori takes advantage, taunting and teasing. Manipulating to get what she wants before dropping them.

I feel bad for Lincoln, watching him as he's unable to keep his eyes off her. He's not like the guys we usually go out with. She could really mess him up if he's not careful.

"*Hello*, Lana," Nina calls to me from the front seat, annoyed.

"Uh, sorry," I respond, realizing I haven't even acknowledged her since getting in the car. "How was your night?"

Nina shrugs. "The usual."

Nina's nineteen. She dropped out of school last year to work at a local strip club. She's tall and thin with straight dark hair that touches her ass, blessed with breasts that men pay to see and pray to touch. She keeps saying she's planning to get her GED. Not sure I believe it.

Nina parties with us when she's not working. She's the type of girl who attracts attention everywhere she goes—supermarket included. Guys are pathetic around her. But she's just as standoffish as we are when it comes to getting serious with anyone. Nina's curse is *Respect*. She demands it from everyone—her friends, her patrons, and especially, her men.

If they disrespect her, she can throw a punch unlike anyone I know. I was surprised the first time I saw it. She nailed some guy in the face for feeling her up while we were at the movies. I'm pretty sure she broke his nose. Nina taught me how to defend myself. Even gave me the small pink switchblade that I have in my pocket.

Nina moved in with Tori after sticking a fork in her mother's boyfriend's thigh. He tried to slide his hand under her skirt while they were eating dinner—*with her mother sitting across the table!* Her mother kicked her out, swearing the man she loved would never have done that. The boyfriend is lucky she didn't aim a little higher. As for her mother ... I have no words.

I'm still not sure why we're in the ogre's car.

Then Nina explains, "So Gary offered to give us a ride and hooked us up with a couple partials." Which means he took some nearly empty bottles of liquor from the club's bar. She raises her eyebrows and her mouth forces into a smile.

Now I know. Gary was our only option, which totally sucks because I'm really not in the mood to put up with his creepy-hand-roaming thing.

"So explain how we got on the list tonight?" Nina asks, still speaking to us through the rearview mirror.

"My brother, Parker," Joey explains.

His fingers casually skim the exposed skin along my waistline. I draw in a quick breath. He must notice because the side of his mouth quirks up, even while he remains focused on Nina's reflection.

Nina whips around in her seat. "Parker Harrison?" Her eyes flit over Joey's face intently, earning a curious look in return.

"You know my brother?" he asks, surprised.

I didn't realize Nina hadn't been told Joey's last name, and she must not have gotten a good look at him 'til now because the relation is pretty obvious.

Nina flashes me a quick glance before turning back around in her seat, composed once again. "We see him out every once in a while," she says, her voice indifferent.

But I know better. Truth is, *everyone* knows who Parker Harrison is. It's hard not to. He's an older, more refined version of Joey. But, unlike Joey, Parker is everywhere—bars, parties, basically anywhere people are having a good time.

Tucking his cell phone in his pocket, Vic leans forward to talk to Gary. "Can we make a stop?"

"This isn't a taxi," Gary gripes. "I didn't know I'd be driving all of *you*." He glares over the seat.

"Aw, Gary," Nina coos, rubbing her slender, manicured fingers on the back of his bulbous head.

I repress a gag. I don't know how she fakes it. There's probably more grease in his slicked hair than in the drip bucket at Stella's.

"You know they're my friends." She leans in close so her shiny red lips are almost touching his ear. "Be nice, please."

Gary sighs in contentment as she pets his huge ogre head. "Where do you want to go?"

"I need to pick up some smokes. Next convenience store works," Vic tells him, sitting back against the seat, his fists clenched within his crossed arms.

What's up with this guy?

"You smell good," Joey says, his nose brushing against my shoulder.

"Thanks," I reply, hoping it's the perfume he's attracted to and not Stella's stench. Thinking back to what Tori said earlier, I try not to laugh. Apparently, grease *is* sexy. That's so wrong.

"I've been wanting to meet you for a while." He squeezes my waist.

I jump and my shoulder knocks him in the jaw.

I cannot believe that just happened.

"I'm so sorry." I cringe, mortified.

"It's okay," he assures me, rubbing his chin. "Didn't realize you were ticklish."

"Very."

"Everywhere?" he asks, a teasing grin spreading on his gorgeous face.

Oh, I wish I could lick that dimple. Yup, I really did just think that.

His other hand grips my thigh. I jump again—without assaulting him this time.

"Guess so," he says with a laugh, gently rubbing the traitorous spot.

If I could whip around and straddle him right now, I would. Slutty, I know. But I swear I'm not usually this pathetic. A guy has *never* affected me like this before. So stop judging.

"I wish we were alone right now," I whisper in his ear, tucking my hand between his knees and running a thumb over his leg.

Okay, fine. Judge. I know we haven't even had a full conversation. But I don't care. I'm sitting on top of the muscular thighs of one of the hottest guys I've ever met, and all I want to do is give in to every urge pulsing through my hormonal teenage body. It's like I have no control.

Joey pulls me in a little closer. "Me too."

"Need another drink?" Tori asks, leaning so far over the front seat that she's practically in my face. "You know, take the edge off?"

She eyes Joey's hand on my bare leg and glares at him. He drops it by his side. I sober with the release of his touch.

"Yeah," I reply guiltily.

*She* knows this isn't me. I'm not the girl who spreads my legs for any guy who looks my way. She usually gives me shit for being so cold and bitchy. Then again, *she's* not sitting on Joey's lap right now, leaning against his firm chest.

Actually, *she's* the reason I'm sitting here!

Tori's almost as small as I am. I could've fit in the front seat of this boat with her and Nina. But she told me to sit in the back with that stupid wink she gave me. So I'm totally blaming my sluttiness on her.

I grab the bottle from her and guzzle until I can't. If tearing off Joey's clothes isn't an option, then I'm going to need a lot of sedation.

I hand the bottle to Joey, who draws in several mouthfuls. I guess I'm not the only one fighting to behave.

We turn into the parking lot of a convenience store with crooked cardboard signs plastered to its grimy windows, advertising cigarettes, milk and lottery tickets. Lincoln slides out of the car after Gary puts it in park. Tori gets out at the same time.

"Why don't I sit in the back? Vic, you can sit up front."

"Whatever," he grumbles, stalking past her and toward the store.

Tori smiles seductively up at Lincoln, brushing her hand along his chest as he holds the door open with the dumbest smile on his face. She's torturing him. And when she ducks into the car, the glint in her eyes tells me she knows it too. Poor guy.

As soon as she scoots next to Joey, she flips my dangling legs up so my feet are on her thighs. "Hey, Lana."

I'm in trouble. And when she clutches my ankle, I know she's definitely not happy with me. Again, this is *her* fault.

"Hey, Tori," I respond, forcing a smile.

Joey looks between us and sinks back into the seat like he's trying to get out of the way.

"You look really cute tonight." She directs her attention to Joey. "Doesn't she look really cute tonight?"

"Uh, yeah," Joey responds, obviously confused and not wanting to be in the middle of whatever this is.

"Thanks," I reply shortly.

Tori is fierce. Not a physical threat like Nina. She and I are barely over five feet. But she has a temper and a vocabulary that makes grown men cower. And when she goes off, her long black curls whip around her head like a raging storm. Her neck flips from side to side, and a finger topped with a sharp nail is in the face of whoever she's telling off. Spanglish snaps from her tongue like a whip, leaving a guy looking for his balls and the most confident girl whimpering. It's like she verbally skins them alive. I've only been on the other end of that Latina finger twice. And neither time ended well.

I watch her hand now, waiting. She keeps it resting on my ankle.

"You should know she's my best friend, Joey." She sounds like one of the guys from the *Godfather* before he pulls out a gun and blows the head off of whoever's across the table from him.

"I *do* know that," Joey replies carefully.

"Then you should know I'm really protective of my friends. Especially my best friend."

He nods. My eyes narrow. I don't get it. Where's this coming from?

"And being with my best friend is *earned*." Tori stares him down. I reach for her hand before she can point the finger. "She's not a prize that lands on your lap. Got it?"

"Of course," he replies, unable to look away from her blazing brown eyes.

"Um, can I talk to you a minute?" I request, squeezing Tori's hand.

She blinks away from Joey and looks to me with a brilliant smile. "Yeah, sure."

I open the door and ease off Joey's lap. Joey moves to get out, and Tori presses her hand into his chest, pushing him back against the seat.

"I got it," she says, crawling around him. She steps out and shuts the door in his face.

"What's up with you? Why are you acting like this?" I ask as soon as we're alone.

"Why are you letting him touch you like that?" she demands. "Lana, that's not you."

"Hey! You're the one who has me sitting on his lap, and if you felt what I felt, you wouldn't be so judgy right now." I clamp my mouth shut, realizing how wrong that sounded.

"You're right. It's my fault," she admits, leaning back against the car with her arms crossed. "I set you up. I should have known you'd be an easy lay for him."

"Yeah, it is your fault! Wait … what? Easy? I'm *not* easy," I say, completely offended. Then I notice the gleam in her eye. She's fucking with me. "You're a bitch, Tori."

"Just needed you to wake up and stop acting like a slut." Tori smiles and steps toward me, pulling me into a hug. "Remember, he's a dumbass guy. He has to deserve you first. You're not a trophy, Lana."

"Right," I reply, suffocated by her mane.

Tori and I made a pact when we were in fifth grade to always be honest and protect each other, no matter what. And then, in sixth grade, after a stupid argument over who could like Justin Walker, we added that no guy is worth fighting over. Ever. Joey Harrison included.

We're interrupted when the back door opens.

"Your phone beeped." Joey has it in his hand.

I take it from him. "Thanks." I pat my jacket pocket and find it open. Thankfully, the switchblade didn't fall out too.

I enter my passcode to read the text from my mother. Could you pick up some flu medicine while you're out?

The flu? I hesitate before responding. We both know this *isn't* the flu. But maybe she just needs something for the symptoms.

I type back, Okay.

Then I slip the phone back in my pocket and zip it up.

"Everything alright?" Joey asks, his brows drawn together in concern.

"Uh"—I force a smile—"I just need to pick up something for my mother. I'll be right back."

I can tell he's about to ask me a question, so I turn away quickly, leaving him standing outside the car, watching me walk away.

I pull open the grime-covered door and freeze after taking just three steps.

I stare at the small silver gun. I don't know what make it is, but it's one of those kinds where the barrel opens up, and the bullets are loaded one at a time. Holding the gun is a big guy wearing a black leather jacket with a scarf pulled up over his nose and a hoodie covering his head.

"What the hell are you doing in here?!" Vic yells at me.

I look from the gun to the skinny man with the bushy mustache behind the counter, his hands raised. I don't say anything.

The guy behind the counter anxiously flips his unblinking eyes between us. I look from him back to Vic. Vic shakes his head at me before focusing on the cashier.

"Hurry up!" Vic yells at the guy, who grabs cash from the register and shoves it across the counter. "And pull out a bunch of lottery tickets too!" Vic demands, forcing his voice to be deeper than it is. "Slowly!" he warns the man.

The cashier reaches his shaking hands to pull at the lottery tickets hanging on the wall behind the counter. He tears off a long string and offers them to Vic.

"Give them to her," Vic demands, waving the gun toward me.

"What?!" I yell. "I don't want anything to do with your dumbass robbery! I'm not touching them."

Vic aims the gun at my chest. "Take the fucking tickets."

I'm not nervous or scared. I'm more annoyed than anything. Why did I have to walk in on this dipwad robbing the convenience store? I bet he's going to walk away with barely two hundred dollars. He's such a fricken idiot.

"Fine." I snatch the trail of tickets from the clerk and fold them up, grumbling, "Asshole," under my breath. I shove them in my inside pocket. "Can we leave now?"

Vic stuffs the bills in his jacket pocket and starts walking backward, keeping the gun pointed at the cashier. I shove the door open and stomp to the car.

"Hurry up and get in the car!" Vic yells at me, hiding the gun in the back of his pants. He pulls down the scarf and shoves back the hood in one quick motion. He's opening the passenger door as I'm sliding back onto Joey's lap. "Drive. Now."

"What just happened?" Gary demands. He's the only one who seems to have noticed our odd exit.

"Nothing," Vic replies, agitated. "Just fucking drive." He looks at me over his shoulder.

I want to punch him in the face. He's beyond stupid! I cross my arms and lean back against the arm Joey has loosely draped around me. I stare Vic down, imagining my hands wrapped around his throat, strangling him.

"Lana, what happened?" Tori asks, easily picking up on my hostile mood.

I don't take my eyes off the contagion that is Vic. I'm certain disdain is written all over my face as I silently curse him with a thousand deaths. I'm not even trying to hide it. But I know, if I say something, everything will go to shit.

"Nothing," Vic snaps.

I don't say a word.

## Chapter Six

*"Lana, why did you punch the boy at school today?" my grandmother asks.*

*"I didn't," I answer honestly.*

*"Who did?"*

*I scrape my foot on the floor, not looking up at her. "My friend."*

*"Why?"*

*"Because he was trying to lift up my skirt." My words are quiet.*

*"Why didn't you say anything when your teacher asked what happened?"*

*"Because I didn't want her to get in trouble."*

*"But you told me."*

*I look up, suddenly afraid. "Is she in trouble?"*

*My grandmother sighs. "No. I would have punched him too."*

After driving maybe five minutes, two cop cars fly by with their lights flashing. I twist around to follow them, my heart racing. When I turn back, Vic is glaring at me.

"Fuck off," I tell him.

Tori and Lincoln look between us and then at each other. Joey's arm circles me protectively.

"Vic, did something happen at the store?" Lincoln asks cautiously.

I'm not sure how well the two of them know each other. But since Joey's not saying anything, Lincoln must feel the need to step up.

"No," Vic grunts.

"Then let me have a cigarette," Gary demands. "You guys are driving me crazy."

Vic remains silent.

"Where are the cigarettes you bought, Vic?" Tori demands, tossing a suspicious look my way before sharing a silent exchange with Lincoln.

"They didn't have my brand," Vic grumbles, his attention directed out the window.

I clench my fists, fighting the urge to scream. This asshat is about to ruin my life, and I need him gone. Now.

"We need to ditch him at the party," I tell Joey, only because his ear is right next to my mouth and Tori's too far away.

"Why?" Joey asks.

I can only shake my head, afraid to say too much and have Vic overhear. As much as I'm not afraid of the douche, he does have a gun. And he's obviously stupid enough to hold up a convenience store with it. He's probably dumb enough to use it too. As much as my life blows, I'm not looking to die tonight.

Everyone knows something's up. The tension in the car is as thick as Gary's neck... which is a tree trunk. Tori keeps staring at the back of Vic's head like she's waiting for him to make a move. Nina starts messing with the music. She may act unfazed, but she'd willingly push him out of the moving car if it came to it.

Lincoln's fighting to remain calm with his hands pressed against his thighs. But the tendons straining in his neck give away just how close he is to losing it.

The only one who seems oddly relaxed is Joey, whose hand has found the skin along my waistband again. Obviously something very wrong is going on, and he hasn't reacted even a little. He's either oblivious or he's brilliant at the whole calm-under-pressure thing.

I'm stiff against him, his touch unable to soothe the tension.

"Can I have the bottle?" I ask Nina.

She slides around and hands me a different bottle of something darker, passing it off with a wink. She's trying to keep me relaxed too. Except I'm not. When I reach for the bottle, my hand is shaking. I resist the urge to crash it over Vic's asinine head.

I swallow down the cinnamon-flavored whiskey until it sends me into a coughing fit. Then I pass the bottle back.

"Someone needs to tell me what the fuck is going on right now, or I'm pulling over and dumping your asses on the side of the road!" Gary bellows over the music, making me flinch.

Joey's grip tightens on my waist.

"No you're not." Vic's voice is low and threatening, like an approaching storm. "Keep driving."

"What did you just say, you little fuck?" Gary's face is redder than raw hamburger, and his skin doesn't look much better.

"Easy, baby," Nina murmurs seductively in his ear.

I shudder when she soothingly runs her hand along the stubble coating the folds of his triple chin.

Joey pulls me back against him. "Don't worry about them." His voice melts me against his hard chest.

I nuzzle into his neck so it looks like I'm kissing him. "How well do you know Vic?"

Joey turns toward me, brushing his fingers along my cheek, our mouths almost touching. His breath tickles as he says, "We're not exactly friends. I told my dad I'd take him out, as a favor."

He pauses and smooths a thumb over my lower lip. Despite this crazy-ass situation, I'm actually getting turned on right now. What is wrong with me?!

"It's … complicated. Why? Did he do something?"

I breathe out slowly, unable to respond.

"Forget about him." He leans in until our lips brush, and I quiver.

"You're fogging up the car," Tori stretches over and says so close, she could join us.

Joey pulls away.

"Tori!" I exclaim, glaring at her.

Tori smirks and sits back again.

I glance behind us, expecting lights to appear at any second. They don't. Or not yet anyway.

"Vic, tell me what you did!" Lincoln suddenly yells, slamming his palm on Vic's headrest.

I jump and Joey presses me against him. He opens his mouth to say something to Lincoln, but then closes it wordlessly.

"I'm sick of your shit. I'm not going down for whatever the fuck you just did! So talk. *Now.*"

I've never heard Lincoln raise his voice before. He's always so calm and put together. But I guess everyone has their limit. And Lincoln's sword is drawn. It's pretty impressive. Tori must think so too because she gives him a once-over with a raised brow.

Vic turns abruptly, leaning over the seat. "Everyone needs to calm the fuck down! Okay? Nothing happened. When Lana walked in, I was yelling at the clerk. He was trying to sell me this shit brand of cigarettes because he didn't have what I wanted. Wouldn't shut up about how they're all the same, and that they'll kill me. I wasn't up for the lecture, so I told him to go fuck himself. When Lana came in, I grabbed her and told her we were leaving. That's why she's acting like she has something stuck up her ass." He directs his attention to me. "Sorry I touched you, okay? Will you just fucking relax?"

Oh, I want to kick him in the face. And I could too, easily, since my foot is dangling off Joey's leg, right below Vic's chin. But before I can, he twists back around and returns to his angry, pouting posture.

"Little boy, you dropped your toy," Nina sings mockingly, displaying the gun on her flat palm.

Just as Vic grabs for it, she flips it in her hand and points it at his forehead.

"Nina!" Tori calls out.

But Nina doesn't react. Her full attention is pinned on Vic.

"You don't know what the fuck you're doing," Vic challenges her.

Nina cocks the hammer.

No one moves. I don't even think we're breathing. Gary may be screaming. But I can't hear him. The entire world is on mute. I'm staring at the silver muzzle indenting the flesh on Vic's skull.

"How do you know it's loaded?" Vic questions, sounding way too cocky for a guy who might have his brains splattered against the window at any second.

"I don't. But you do," she says, her shiny red lips parting to reveal a big white smile.

"You know I could take that from you, right?"

Nina just smirks wickedly. I grimace with a silent groan. Vic better shut his mouth. He has no idea who he's talking to.

Nina's a fighter. I'm convinced she came into the world that way so she could survive the shit she's been dealt her entire life. She may look super girlie and have a figure to die for, but she's ferocious. Without hesitation, she's had my back in a fight more times than I can count. Even when I'm the one who started it.

So I know, if Vic makes a move, I'm going to want to block my ears.

The car stops. At least it doesn't feel like we're moving anymore. I'm afraid to look away to find out.

"Nina, honey, would you please put down the gun?" Gary asks her so gently, it doesn't even sound like him.

My eyes remain glued to the point where the gun is attached to Vic's head. His jaw tenses. Nina smiles wider, a menacing glint in her dark eyes.

"What did you do in the store?" Nina asks calmly.

Vic swallows. "Nothing. Ask Lana."

"I'm not asking her. I'm asking *you*. She's a sweet girl, and she shouldn't be involved in this. She might actually go to college. I'm not fucking with that. I'm not going to let *you* fuck with that either. So, one more time. What did you do in that convenience store?"

Vic sneers. "Nothing."

"Okay, I'm going to shit myself if you don't put down the gun, Nina! Please!" Gary whimpers.

I steal a glance his way. Beads of sweat are covering his forehead and streaking down the sides of his face. He may even be crying. My nose scrunches in disgust. I know this is intense, but … really?

"Fine," Nina huffs and tips the gun back, easing the hammer in place.

The entire car exhales.

"Give me my gun," Vic demands, holding out his hand.

Nina laughs. "Uh. No."

"Get out!" Gary screams. "Get out of my car! Now!" He opens his door.

The next thing I know, my door is open and he's yanking me out.

"Hey!" I holler, trying to pull my arm out of his clammy grip.

"All of you, out! I'm not putting up with this shit!"

I yank free, but the force of the motion sends me tripping over my four-inch wedges, and I topple onto my ass. Joey is out a second later, followed by Tori, both of them in Gary's face. The finger is out, and Spanish flies from Tori's mouth.

"Keep your hands off her!" Joey yells, practically bumping against Gary's gut. He's taller than Gary by a few inches, but Gary wins with three times the girth.

A large black hand is in my face. I look up. It takes me a couple seconds to realize that Lincoln is offering to help me up.

"Thanks."

His hand completely swallows mine as he lifts me off the ground. I swipe at the dirt on my butt, still watching the three go at it. It's all words. Nothing about their posture has me concerned that someone's about to swing.

We're in the middle of nowhere. There's maybe a streetlight every quarter mile on this forgotten road, lighting it just enough to make it creepy. Gary pulled off into one of those gravel turnouts on the side of the road—the ideal location when you're desperate to relieve your bladder or throw your door open just in time to vomit. So not the ideal location to be dumped with a psycho and his gun.

"Where's Nina and Vic?" I ask in a rush, frantically searching the darkness.

"I don't know," Lincoln answers, his voice as concerned as mine.

We creep toward the front of the car. Nina's back is to us. She's leaning against the fender on the other side of the car. Vic is in his signature angry stance, scowling at her.

Nina has the barrel of the gun open and is *throwing* bullets at Vic.

"Tell me what you did, Vic," she says in a taunting tone. "C'mon. You want your toy back, don't you?"

Vic grunts something.

"Then tell me. Quit being a bitch." There's a sadistic lilt in Nina's voice, like she's enjoying this.

She's starting to scare me a little. I put a big star on that mental note I already had, reminding me to never piss her off.

Vic bares his teeth. "Give me my gun, or I'm going to—"

"To what?" Lincoln challenges, straightening a few inches taller, like he might jump over the car.

Vic looks up and spots us across the hood. Nina snaps the barrel shut with a flick of her wrist and stuffs the gun into her purse.

Vic breathes out audibly, like he can't believe he has to repeat himself. "This is a fucking joke. I don't know why you won't drop it. *Nothing* happened."

At least he's persistent with the nothing-happened story. I have to give him that. And I'm not going to contradict it. If I do, everyone in the car could be considered accomplices after the fact. And I won't let that happen. Right now, only Vic and I know what went down in that store. And we're the only ones who will ever know. Unless he does something else stupid.

Nina approaches us with a hip-swaying saunter. The dark purple dress hugs her curves perfectly as she balances on heels that bring her to supermodel height. She looks completely unfazed by everything that just transpired. A lethal goddess.

If only I were that composed ... and tall.

"Screw this," Gary declares loudly. "Nina, let's go."

Nina shakes her head with an insincere apology. "Sorry, baby. I'm staying."

"But you said—"

"I lied," she interrupts.

Gary growls, furious. "Don't bother showing up tomorrow."

Nina doesn't flinch.

Before any of us can react, Gary is in the car, reversing with the gas pedal pressed to the floor. Joey jumps out of the way to avoid getting clipped. Shifting to drive, Gary tears off down the street, covering us in a spray of gravel.

Waving my hand to clear the dust storm, I watch the taillights disappear in disbelief. "What the hell?! My bag's in his car."

Which means my house keys are too. I reach into my open jacket pocket, relieved to find I still have my phone and switchblade.

"I can't believe he just left us here." Tori has her hands on her hips. Looking around the dark, deserted road, she asks, "Where are we?"

"I think we're still a few miles away." Lincoln lifts his hand as if to touch her back, then stops himself and lowers it.

"There's no way I'm walking in these," she says, gesturing to her knee-high boots. She whips around and points a bladed nail at Vic. "Why do you have to be such an asshole? I swear—"

"What? She's the one who held the gun to my head." Vic jerks his chin aggressively toward Nina. "I didn't do anything wrong."

"Except have a gun to begin with!" Tori screams, her curls flailing.

"I brought it for protection," Vic argues.

"From *us*? You're fucking unbelievable."

Nina wraps an arm around Tori's shoulders, coaxing her away before it can escalate further. I turn my back to them, needing to escape the drama.

"You okay?" Joey asks, coming up beside me.

"Not even a little," I reply, taking a few steps toward the edge of the road.

He slips his arm around my waist, easing my back against him to shield me from everyone behind us. Tucking his thumb into the top of my shorts, he rests his chin on the top of my head. "Let's work on that. What do you think?"

I laugh lightly. "Go for it. Anything you can do to make this night better, I'm in." But I already feel better leaning into him. I'm convinced I could block out bombs going off—all he has to do is touch me and whisper in my ear.

I'm suddenly spun around, Joey's hands firmly gripping my hips. As aggressive as the move was, his lips don't crash down on mine. Instead they tease, barely touch. I'm breathless. I grab him by the back of the neck to pull him into me.

"Joey, give your brother a call. Maybe he can send someone to pick us up."

Yup. We're still not alone.

I ease away, my breath caught in my chest. I look around to find everyone staring at us.

Tori tilts her head to the side, not amused. "Stop groping her and get us a ride."

"There isn't a signal at The Point," Joey tells them.

Lincoln releases a heavy breath. "Shit, that's right."

"So what do we do?" I ask. I turn at the sound of a car approaching.

"Screw this," Tori says, striding out past the white line and halfway into the lane with her hip thrust out.

The headlights illuminate her fitted black shorts and sheer top over a hot-pink bra. She waves her arms in the air. They're either going to hit her or …

They swerve, missing her, and then slow to a stop along the side of the road.

"Nice," Lincoln says, impressed.

Actually, so am I.

The red pickup truck backs up, braking a few feet away.

"How do we know they're not psychos?" I ask.

"We don't," Tori says. "But we have our own psycho, so if anything, *they* should be worried." She looks toward Vic. Except he's not here. "Where'd our psycho go?"

"Vic!" Lincoln calls out.

But he doesn't appear from within the shadows of the trees where he was sulking only a moment ago.

The driver's window rolls down, and a guy with super gelled dark blond hair leans out. "Need a lift?"

Lincoln steps forward. "Yeah, man, that'd be great. Our ride ditched us. We're trying to get to The Point."

"Us too!" a voice squeals excitedly.

That's when I notice the girl with a hot-pink bobbed wig sticking her head out the small window in the back of the cab. Her face is speckled with glitter, and she's smiling so big, she's making my cheeks hurt looking at her.

"You can jump in the back," the guy tells us.

Lincoln looks around again as we near the truck. "Vic!"

"Leave him," Nina says, pulling out a bottle from her satchel of a purse. She approaches the passenger side and waves the liquor at the girl. "Can I sit up here with you?"

"Sure!" the girl exclaims. "Wow. You're so nice. Look, Seth, she's sharing with us." She scoots over to make room for Nina. "I'm Allie."

"Great," Nina replies. She tips the bottle back and chugs, preparing herself to sit next to the happiest girl on the planet.

Joey and Lincoln lower the tailgate and hop into the back before offering to help Tori and me up.

Just as Lincoln reaches to close it again, Vic's fingers curl around the metal, forcing it back down. "Hey!"

"Where were you?" Lincoln asks him in alarm. "Didn't you hear me calling you?"

"What the hell, man? Were you going to leave me?" Vic jumps up onto the truck and shoves Lincoln.

Joey leaps forward to get between them. "Don't start." His voice is low and authoritative.

No one moves. Joey looks between the two guys. Their eyes lock, silently challenging each other.

"Sit down."

Lincoln backs away and sits, resting against the cab without taking his eyes off Vic. Joey lowers himself beside me, prepared to jump back up if necessary. Vic stands defiantly, glaring at Lincoln with his fists clenched.

"Vic, sit your ass down," I tell him.

He directs his attention to me, trying to intimidate me with his scary stare. I roll my eyes. He grabs the edge of the tailgate to close it.

Tori knocks on the window. "We can go."

Vic stumbles and falls on his ass when the truck takes off. I snicker. If only he'd fallen out.

## Chapter Seven

*"Don't lose yourself to anyone," my aunt Allison says to me, lying on her bed, staring up at the ceiling with a funny-smelling cigarette dangling between her fingers, "not a boy or a friend or even your family. You can't care what anyone thinks of you, Lana, because as soon as you do, you're lost."*

Joey leans back against the cab and eases me onto his lap. "I like you here."

"I like me here too," I admit, relaxing against his chest.

"How are you doing now?" he asks, his breath tickling my neck.

"Better." I smile.

He smiles back, revealing the dimple. I lean over and kiss it. I can't help myself. Joey turns his head and his lips barely brush across mine. Shooting stars surge through my entire body.

He hasn't truly kissed me yet, and the anticipation is causing my pulse to beat erratically. Seriously, I need ten minutes … twenty alone with him and we'll both be soaring. All the crazy that's happened tonight will instantly be forgotten.

Joey presses his forehead against mine. "What do you think about starting over? You know, have tonight start right now?"

"I think I like that," is released within a breath.

Joey caresses my cheek with his thumb, eliciting a shiver.

Out of the corner of my eye, I notice big blue eyes right next to my head. I lean back to find Allie's face poking through the cab window, her chin resting on her hand, staring at us dreamily.

"You two are so cute."

Tori snorts loudly. I flip her the finger.

"Here." Allie offers me the nearly depleted bottle of liquor.

I take it from her, down a shot and pass it off. I've been waiting for the buzz to kick in, to mellow me out. But this night has been anything but chill. Hopefully it will finally overtake me when we get to The Point.

"You guys know that The Point parties are exclusive, right?" Joey announces to everyone in the bed of the truck. "We're not really supposed to have access, so keep it between us. Okay?" He focuses on Vic, receiving an affirming grunt in return.

"Of course," Tori assures him.

"We won't say anything," I promise. "How do people usually get on the list?"

"All I know is that everyone on the list has to be approved. I'm not sure how they request to get on it. But they have to pay crazy money for the privilege, basically ensuring their silence, or else they're blackballed—which, in this group, is social suicide."

"How do they find out about the parties?" I ask.

I've been *dying* to go since I first found out about The Point parties two years ago. We've only ever heard whispers *after* they've happened—the secrecy heightening my obsession.

"Everyone on the list receives a text with a code on it. When they sign in, the location is revealed along with a bar code that gets them in. They can pay to bring up to six of their friends." As an afterthought, Joey adds, "Oh, phones aren't allowed inside. You have to check them in as you enter."

"Who came up with this? It's insane," I ask, impressed.

"No one knows. The organizers don't want anyone knowing their identities so they can't be influenced, or busted. This isn't exactly legal," Joey explains. "I heard they've expanded it to six different spots in three towns. I think they're trying to make it a legit business."

Tori eyes him suspiciously. "How do you know so much about it?"

Joey only shrugs with a grin that convinces me he knows someone involved.

I sink back against the side of the truck, groaning. "Wait. How much does it cost to get in? I don't have a ton of money on me." I can't waste my tip money on a party, not if I want to keep our lights on.

"You're with me tonight," Joey says, taking hold of my hand. "Don't worry about it."

"You sure?" I ask, uncomfortable with him paying.

"Very." Joey pulls me closer to him and lowers his voice, his mouth next to my ear. "But this isn't our first date, Lana. I want to save that for another night, okay? Because I definitely want to see you again."

It sounds like a line. I should totally blow him off like I do any other guy who tries too hard. Except it doesn't *feel* like a line. Everything about him makes my heart race, causing me to do and say things I never would.

I press my lips together to hide the huge smile that wants to explode onto my face. "I want to see you again too." I am *so* pathetic tonight.

We pull through the open gates of the chain-link fence a few minutes later, entering The Point—which is a collection of old brick factory buildings and warehouses in the middle of nowhere. Some of the buildings are abandoned. Others have businesses in them. It's hard to tell the difference because they all look like they should be torn down.

The truck stops at the first building. "We'll let you off here since we have to park out back."

"Thanks for the ride," Lincoln tells him as Nina gets out of the cab and shuts the door.

"Not a problem."

"We'll look for you inside." Allie pops out of the open window and sits on the door. "Love you guys!" She remains hanging out of the truck when Seth pulls away, thrusting her arms in the air and screaming in excitement.

"What is she on?" Tori asks.

"Sunshine and fucking rainbows," Nina says, grabbing the bottle away from Lincoln.

I laugh.

"Girl talk," Tori says to Joey and Lincoln.

They nod in understanding and start walking down the alley between the first and second buildings. Vic remains behind us ... somewhere. I should probably be more aware of where he is. I should also be more afraid of him than I am. But I'm not.

Tori nudges me with her shoulder to get my attention. "About earlier ... I know how weird you can get about keeping your mouth shut, especially if you think it might take us down too. I won't ask. But know you have nothing to worry about. Okay?"

"We've got you," Nina pledges, passing me the bottle. "And I'll get your bag from Gary tomorrow because you know he can't fire me."

I look between her and Tori. "Thanks."

"Now what's up with you and Joey?" Nina asks giddily.

"I'm not sure," I answer honestly. "But whatever it is, it's ... intense. I can't explain it."

"Yeah. Anyone within ten feet of you two can smell the *intensity*." Tori shoots me a side-eyed look loaded with judgment. She takes the bottle from me.

"Ew, Tori," Nina says with a laugh.

"Stop. I'm not going to hook up with him. But let me have a little fun, okay?" I implore.

Tori lifts a shoulder in resignation.

"Speaking of fun"—I reach into my pocket and pull out the plastic bag—"look what I got us for tonight. It only cost me ... well, nothing."

Nina squeals. "Let me see." She examines the bag in her palm. "There's a little of everything in here. They sell it like this?"

"They call it, 'party in a bag.'"

"That's kind of a stupid and genius name at the same time," she says, pulling the seal apart and selecting a tiny foil square labeled with a smiling mushroom sticker. "Do you trust them?"

"Can you really trust anyone with a pocketful of drugs?"

"True," Nina replies. "Well, here goes nothing." She chews the chocolate and swallows. "Let the party begin."

"Don't get lost on your trip," Tori tells Nina, taking the bag from her. She removes the small blue pill with an *X* stamped on it before handing the bag back to me.

I inspect the contents, select the brown powder capsule of Molly and toss it back with a swig from the bottle, finally starting to feel the mellowing effects of the alcohol.

"This night is going to be ridiculous!" Nina exclaims, thrusting her arms in the air with an exaggerated sway of her hips.

"Now how do we get rid of Psycho?" I tip my head slightly in Vic's direction.

"We'll lose him inside," Tori assures me. "But don't go anywhere alone. I don't trust him."

Joey and Lincoln have stopped at the end of the next building, waiting for us.

"It's insane how much he looks like Parker." Nina scans Joey, eyeing him like he's candy.

"Which is why I'm a little creeped out about you two together," Tori says to me. "But I'll lay off, I promise."

Tori hands Lincoln the bottle when we reach them. The guys finish off the last of it and toss it in a dumpster across the alley.

I notice a group of people enter a blue door farther down.

"Is that where we're going?" Nina asks.

"Yeah, that's our entrance," Joey tells us.

"There's more than one?" I'm still trying to wrap my head around this setup.

"They don't want lines outside to give away the location, so there are five entrances, and everyone's given a block of time to show up. They also need to keep us hidden from the cops."

"You seriously know a lot about this for someone who's never been," Tori notes, studying him warily.

Joey doesn't respond.

When we reach the door, Joey takes my hand. "I don't want to lose you."

I give him a gentle squeeze back, not planning on being lost.

The door cracks open, revealing a hint of the broad figure behind it. Joey releases my hand long enough to pull out his phone and bring up the code. The guy scans it with another phone, and the image disappears.

"How many?"

"Five."

"Six," Vic corrects him.

Joey's back stiffens. It's the first time I've seen him react to Vic or any of the fucked-up-ed-ness that's happened tonight.

Joey shakes his head in annoyance and says, "Six."

The door opens and we're ushered into a tight hallway. The guy locks the outside door behind us.

"Phones." The guy holds out a black plastic bag.

Reluctantly, I drop mine inside, followed by everyone else. He hands a token to Joey, who slips it into his front pocket.

"Hands," the doorman demands.

Joey holds out his hand, turning it over. The guy presses a stamp against the back of his wrist. I do the same, letting him brand me with ultraviolet ink.

Once he's marked everyone, he unlocks the black door at the other end of the hallway and silently holds it open. The whole man-of-a-few-words thing he has going on is intimidating. It could also be the six-ish feet of bulging muscle. I doubt anyone's stupid enough to mess with him. And just as the thought enters my head, Vic tries to push past us, practically knocking me over.

The doorman shoves him against the wall. "Cut the shit or you're out."

Joey's hands are on my waist, steadying me. "You okay?"

I nod.

"Vic, stay the fuck away from us," Nina threatens.

We move past him, his dark eyes following us as we enter a dimly lit stairwell. A giant pink neon arrow points up, so we do as instructed and climb the stairs. I feel the bass pounding above us before I can hear the music. On the next level, a green neon star marks a red door. As soon as Joey opens it, we're engulfed by electronic beats and lasers cutting across the room.

We step inside. The door falls shut behind us as we stare in wordless wonder. I've never been to anything like this before. I can't move for a minute, needing to take it all in. The entire space is surrounded by large screens, displaying images and colors pulsing to the music. The DJ is at the far end on an elevated stage—a bouncing silhouette between a lit booth and a wall of screens. It's what I imagine a club in Vegas or LA would be like. And to think they set this up for one night in an abandoned building is beyond insane.

"I can't believe I'm here," I utter in awe.

Everywhere I look, people are dancing, even along the mezzanine that wraps around the upper level.

Joey turns to me, his eyes lit with excitement. "Ready?" He offers me his hand, eager to get lost in the crowd.

I laugh. "Yes." Taking his outstretched hand, I let him navigate us toward the stage.

I glance over my shoulder to make sure Nina, Lincoln and Tori are behind us.

"Go!" Nina yells after me, still by the door.

When I realize they aren't following, I pull Joey back toward them.

"We'll find you after we go to the bar."

"Will you hold my jacket then?" I ask her, already feeling too warm. Shrugging out of it, I toss it to Nina before they disappear in the opposite direction.

Joey clasps my hand again, and within a few feet, we're swallowed up by the crowd of jumping, swaying and grinding bodies.

When we're completely immersed somewhere in the middle of the madness, he turns to me and places his hands on my hips, drawing me to him. "We'll get a drink in a little while. I've needed this all night."

I drape my hands over his shoulders and lose myself to the bass, rolling with the wave of intoxication that has finally taken over. With his hands gripping my hips, Joey guides our bodies until they're moving in unison. He's really good at this. Maybe *too* good because I'm so overwhelmed by the feel of him against me that everyone else disappears. His hands glide from my hips to the small of my back, pressing me firmly against him. If we were any closer, we'd dissolve into each other.

I've never wanted a guy this badly before. Then again, a guy's never made me *feel* like this before. My body responds to his slightest touch. My pulse quickens every time his voice rumbles low in my ear. I'm held captive by him—willingly. I could seep into his skin and lose myself.

Joey dips his head down and slides his mouth along my neck. I draw in a quick breath. When he reaches my lips, he breathes against them, continuing to tease and torment me. I close my eyes, needing to taste him, but he refuses to kiss me. I exhale slowly, unraveling.

A few songs later, a tap on the shoulder wakes me from my Joey-induced haze. Tori is standing next to us with Lincoln and Nina dancing behind her. We separate to include them. Nina hands me a bottle of water with a knowing wink, and I could kiss her. My mouth is so dry, it's like I've swallowed sand.

Every so often Joey brushes his hand against mine, playfully interlacing our fingers. I know he's trying not to give Tori a reason to throw her drink on him. But it's too hard for us to resist. We're overcome with a compulsion to touch. Within a song, he surrenders to the pull, moving in close behind me. I wrap my arms around his neck, and he trails his hand down my side. Our bodies ease together in a fluid, singular motion.

"I think I need a drink," Joey murmurs in my ear before tasting the sweat on my neck.

I squeeze his hands on my hips. "Yeah, me too." I look to Tori and Nina. "Bar?"

They nod and we cut through the crowd to the other end of the open space.

Just when the dancers start to thin out, we run into a wall of people waiting to order drinks at the glowing square bar.

"There you are!" I look back to see a hand on Joey's shoulder. "I thought I told you to stay downstairs when you got here and I'd come give you your keys."

I turn to find Parker Harrison standing before us.

Parker and Joey may look alike in many ways, but while Joey's disheveled and sexy, Parker's polished and powerful. Joey's hair is displaced from raking his fingers through it, and Parker's is trimmed and neatly parted to the side. Joey's boyishly charming in an untucked button-down while Parker's jaw-droppingly kempt in a sports jacket. He looks ... important.

I find myself captivated by eyes the same shade of electric blue as the boy I've been grinding against for the past hour. But I don't expect the betrayal I see reflected back in them. Whatever lecture he was about to give his brother about being here is lost.

"Lana? What are you doing here?"

"Hi, Parker." My stomach twists when his focus darts from Joey to me in confusion.

"You know each other?" Joey asks.

"Yeah," Parker replies, sounding distant as he pins me with a questioning stare.

I don't say anything. There isn't anything to say. But I don't look away either, even though I should.

"Lana's here with me tonight."

I can feel the weight of Joey's arm around my shoulder, claiming me.

Parker tears his attention away from me and gives his brother a pitying look. Then he laughs this amused, almost maniacal laugh. "Are you sure about that?"

"Hey, Parker." Nina steps between us, stopping directly in front of him, her chest brushing against his. "Buy me a drink?"

Parker eases his hand along her waist and places a ghost of a kiss on her cheek. "Hey, gorgeous. Maybe later? I have to go take care of something."

Nina visibly deflates but recovers quickly. "No problem."

Lengthening her spine, she turns and walks briskly away. I almost shiver from the ice rolling off her.

I step out from under Joey's territorial limb and follow after her. Tori comes up beside me and makes a pained face when I look at her.

"I know, right?! What the hell was that about?" I huff.

But Tori's expression doesn't change. Clearly she's not listening. She runs a knuckle under her eye, indicating I should do the same.

I swipe my finger to remove the smeared makeup. "Better?"

Tori shakes her head with a grimace, like it hurts her to see me like this. "You're a mess."

I'm suddenly afraid to know what I look like. I glance down at the rivulets of sweat running down my chest, disappearing into my cleavage, forming dark blue wet marks under my boobs. Tori's right. I'm a disaster.

"I'll be right back," I tell her, needing to disappear immediately.

She nods, hurrying me past her.

"Lana!" Joey calls after me.

"Relax. She's just going to the bathroom," I hear Tori tell him. "You can live without her for ten minutes."

I spot flashing neon lights in the left corner, animating a girl dancing. There's one of a guy fist-pumping directly across from it. They have to be the bathrooms.

I swipe my fingers under my eyes again and keep my head down, not wanting anyone to see the mascara melting down my face.

An arm wraps around my waist and I'm swept into the darkness under the stairs.

"Why are you here with my brother?"

"Holy shit, Parker!" I exclaim breathlessly, lowering the elbow that was inches from smashing his nose.

"Tell me," he demands impatiently, remaining way too close. I attempt to take a step back, but his arm tightens around my waist. "You've refused to go out with me every time I've asked. My brother's home for a day and you're here with *him*?"

"Really?" I huff, pushing at his chest to separate us.

Parker releases me and gestures impatiently when I don't continue.

"Lincoln asked Tori to a party tonight. And it turns out, Lincoln and Joey are friends, which I'm sure you know. We're all here together. But it's not like you have any claim. You know that."

"Why do you have to be so difficult?"

Parker takes a step toward me, and I mimic it with a step back.

"You know why." It's a conversation we've had too many times over the past year, and my answer's not going to change.

"I don't have to see her again. You know what it's like with her. We're not *together*," he pleads. "We use each other. That's it."

"And that makes it better? She's one of my best friends. You became untouchable to me the moment you touched her. You know my rule."

I know what the two of them have doesn't mean anything. Nina pretty much repeats the same thing Parker just said. But they still get together, no matter how toxic whatever they have is. *Respect* and *Confidence*—like fire and an accelerant, their curses are a dangerous combination. They're constantly tearing each other apart—when they're not ... well, tearing each other apart.

He growls in frustration. "Don't start anything with my brother." His words have an underlying threat to them.

"What?! You don't have a say in that either!"

"Lana, don't ... " Before he can finish whatever asinine thing he's about to say, I clench my teeth to keep from screaming and stalk past him. "Lana!"

"Stay away from me, Parker!" I yell over my shoulder, hurriedly squeezing by people to increase the distance between us. My shoulder collides with a body.

"Lana?"

I slowly look up to find a guy with wavy brown hair and big dark eyes looking down at me. I scan the mold of the navy T-Shirt over his sculpted chest and the way his snug jeans fit perfectly. He's hot. Then I meet his eyes again and realize who he is. Holy shit.

"Mr. Garner?"

I instantly want to die. I just thought my guidance counselor was *hot*. But, in my defense, he looks way different without the glasses and tie. *Way* different.

"Isaac," he corrects quickly, looking around like we might get caught doing something wrong. "What are you doing here?" Before I can answer, he says, "Forget it. Where's Tori?"

I tip my head toward the line at the bar. He looks in her direction and nods, even though she's hidden within the crowd.

"I can't believe you're here," he says, shaking his head. "Actually, if any of my students could get into this place, it'd be you and Tori. I swear it'll be a miracle if you two graduate in one piece."

I often think the same thing. "Wasn't expecting to see *you* either."

"You probably don't know, but I grew up in Oaklawn. I went to school with a lot of people here."

"How old are you?" I ask automatically.

I always thought he was old, like thirty or something. Maybe it's the tie ... or seeing him sitting behind a desk, surrounded by inspirational quotes. But tonight, dressed like a normal guy, he doesn't look much older than ... Parker.

"Old enough to know I shouldn't be caught drinking with you," he replies. "I didn't see you tonight. And you didn't see me."

"I don't even know who you are," I say, which isn't far from the truth.

*Isaac* laughs. Even thinking his first name feels wrong. "Be good, Lana. Don't get into trouble." Then he walks off.

Talk about weird. This night cannot get any more twisted. And just as I think it, I wish I hadn't. The last thing I want to do is tempt Fate. We don't have a good history.

"Hey! There you are! I thought I'd lost you. Wait. Where are the rest of your friends? Are you lost? Do you need me to help you find them?"

I remain still, staring up at the willowy girl with bright pink hair in a turquoise bandeau and matching sequined miniskirt.

"It's Allie!"

"Umm, yeah. I remember." Like there's any way I could possibly forget. "They're in line at the bar. I have to use the bathroom."

"Me too!" she exclaims. "I found this super-secret bathroom upstairs that doesn't have a line. Wanna come?!"

I eye the football field length line waiting to get in the girls' bathroom. "Sure."

Allie takes my hand and leads me up the stairs to the mezzanine level. Looking down from here, I can see how big this place truly is. It's crazy-huge. The space is lined with black curtains, making it feel more private and ...

sinister. I watch a girl in a metallic dress disappear into the dark with a bottle and glasses on her tray. It takes a moment for my eyes to adjust before I see the groups of people on lush couches concealed within the shadows. I can only imagine what they're doing back there.

"So there's this office or something hidden up here with a bathroom in it. Another girl showed me earlier," Allie tells me.

She pulls back a section of the heavy curtain next to a black door, casting light into the dark space. I quickly duck through the opening and she follows, concealing us behind the fabric wall.

Light shines through a window-lined office where four girls wait to use the bathroom. When we enter, the first thing I notice is an oversized ornate mirror propped on a metal desk. A girl's leaning in close to it, lining her eyes. When I approach it, I immediately cringe at my reflection. No wonder Joey hasn't kissed me.

I slide my headband off and let my hair down, shaking out the sweat-soaked strands. I rake my fingers through the length that extends to my lower back before sweeping it up into a large twisted bun and securing it on top of my head, sliding the crystal headband back in place. That's a *little* better.

"Is your hair white?" Allie asks.

I turn with a start, unaware she was hovering.

"It's blond. It's just really light."

She's not the first to mistake my hair for being white. Although it's usually little kids I'm correcting.

"You should totally color it white," she says to my reflection, stepping closer to the mirror without blinking her eyes. "You would look like a frost princess. But you really *do* look like a princess." She reaches out to touch me, the reflected me, running a finger along my headband. "It's so sparkly."

"Uh, thanks. My mother gave it to me." I watch her curiously. She's definitely ... unique.

Allie spins around to face me, the real me, and throws her arms around my neck. "You're *so* beautiful," she says, hugging me tight. She steps back, holding me at arm's length, and just stares at me like she's trying to decide if I'm real. "I'm so high."

I nod. Really? I mean, the wide, unblinking eyes pretty much gave that away. And for the first time, I recognize I'm feeling pretty floaty myself—but definitely not lost in the stratosphere like Allie.

"You gotta go?" a thin brunette in boy shorts and a bikini top asks, motioning toward the bathroom that just opened up.

"I do," I answer. And I also need the sink to clean off the black streaks running down my face. I look like I've been crying mud.

I ease out of Allie's grip and enter the bathroom.

When I come back out, Allie's still there. I'm not sure why. Maybe she thinks we're friends now. Except ... we're not.

I inspect the sweat marks on my top in the mirror. Pulling the fabric away from my skin, I flap it gently, hoping it'll dry.

"Want to go outside?" Allie asks. "It's so hot in here." She plops down on the desk, like she's too weak to stand. "I need some air."

She doesn't look so good. I'm worried she may pass out, and there's no way I can hold her up.

"Where can we go?"

"This way," she says, crisscrossing her long legs as she weaves toward the door. "Why am I so hot? This is so not good, my princess."

"It's okay," I assure her, taking her by the elbow to steer her through the curtain so that she doesn't grab on to it and pull it down. "Which way?"

"That way." Allie points right.

I direct us through the black door, entering a stairwell.

"That way again." Her finger indicates a blue door with *Exit* lit above it.

I push through and find a small group of people smoking on a fire escape spanning the alley between two buildings.

Allie stumbles out of my grasp and trots down a few feet before collapsing on a grated metal step. "Omigod. My skin needed this so bad." She flops her arms over the railing in blissful relief.

"Water?" some guy asks, offering her a bottle.

"You are so super sweet," she says, looking up at him with her big blue eyes and thousand-watt smile.

I grab the bottle from him first to make sure it's sealed before letting her have it.

When she dumps half of it in her mouth, she releases an obnoxiously loud moan. "Best. Water. Ever."

"Glad I could make you happy," the guy says with a creepy, predator smile.

I turn to him, knowing he's lingering because he thinks he has a chance with her. "Get lost."

He scowls and goes back into the building. That's when I notice the black boots on the steps next to my head. And, of course, I find Vic, the master scowler, doing exactly that down at me.

I let out a disgusted breath and focus on Allie, pointedly ignoring him. "How are you feeling?"

"I'm so happy," she responds, beaming. "Here, have some." She hands me the bottle of water before taking ahold of the railing to pull herself up.

I easily finish it and abandon the empty bottle on the step. "Thanks."

Allie stares at me with that same doe-eyed expression she wore in the truck. "You could be a fairy, you know. You have the biggest black eyes."

"They're brown."

"A little, tiny nose, kissed with stardust."

"Or freckles."

"And super-pointy cheekbones. Do you have pointy ears too?"

She tips her head to look, like she expects they might be.

"I don't."

"All you need are wings and you'd be my fairy princess." She places her palms on my cheeks and speaks in a high-pitched voice, "I wish I could shrink you and put you in my pocket."

I have no idea what she's talking about. She's delusional. I need to get her back to her boyfriend.

"Where's Seth? Let's go find him. I'm sure my friends are wondering where I am too." Or at least I hope they are.

"You do have wings! They're just hiding!" Allie declares when I turn to walk toward the door. She traces a finger along my right shoulder blade. "You *are* my fairy princess!"

"Yup, you're right," I say with a sigh.

When I glance at her over my shoulder, I realize Vic is gone—which is a good and bad thing. Good because I can't stand to be within two feet of him. Bad because now I have no idea where he is again, and I still don't trust him not to do something stupid.

I reach for the door at the same time it pushes open. A girl steps out and I slide by her.

"Allie!" I hear her screech in excitement right before the door clicks shut behind me.

I groan into the empty stairwell, knowing Allie's no longer following me. I'd much rather be drinking and dancing with my friends, but I can't leave her. She's a disaster. I have to help her find Seth. I'm blaming the drugs for my uncharacteristic kindness.

I set my hand on the release bar. As the door cracks open, I'm forcefully yanked from behind and slammed against the wall. Pain floods my head when it collides with the concrete. I blink to clear the spots from my eyes, disoriented. Something hard pokes my ribs and a forearm presses against my chest, pinning me. I pull at the arm, then grunt when the object jabs into me. It's a gun.

How many guns does he have? Did he get this back from Nina? Why am I thinking about this right now?

"You're not going to say anything about what happened tonight," Vic demands, his rank breath invading my senses.

I stab him a thousand times with my glare. When I refuse to answer, he thrusts his weight against me, crushing my chest. I grit my teeth in pain.

"Right?"

"I'm not going to say anything," I growl. "Now get off me!"

I try to push him, but he shoves me back against the concrete, banging my head again. I cry out, overcome with blinding pain.

"If you do, I'll hurt you," he threatens. "I mean, *really* hurt you."

"Hey! Get off my fairy princess!" Before I can react, Allie jumps on Vic's back. "Leave her alone!"

"What the— Get off me, you psycho!" Vic bellows as she wraps an arm around his neck and pounds his back with her fist.

Vic steps back. I move to get out from under his arm, but he lunges forward, trapping me again. He whips the hand holding the gun over his shoulder and hits Allie on the side of the head.

"Ow!" she yelps, releasing him and landing with a hard thud on her feet. She staggers backward, her hand cradling her head. "That hurt."

"You asshole!" I jam my knee between his legs.

Vic moans in pain and bends in half, cupping himself. Clasping my hands together, I swing up as hard as I can, colliding with his jaw. Vic's head flips up with a howl. He stumbles back, slamming into Allie.

Allie pounds his arm with the sides of her fists. "You're so mean!"

Vic reaches out and clutches Allie by the throat. She claws at his hand, making gurgling noises. As I rush toward him, he stares at me, his dark brows dipping to shadow his eyes. A malevolent, bloody smile creeps across his face, causing me to falter in my steps. If evil has a face, he's staring at me right now. I know exactly what he's about to do the second before he does it.

"No!"

I reach for Allie ... just as Vic tosses her down the stairs.

## Chapter Eight

*"Where's my daddy?" I ask.*

*Everyone stops eating. My aunt Allison's fork clangs on her plate. I look at my mom. She doesn't say anything.*

*"He's gone, baby girl," my grandmother tells me, running her hand over my head.*

*A sharp cry escapes and my mom cups a hand over her mouth to trap it as tears fill her eyes. She looks like she's in so much pain.*

*I never ask about my dad again.*

Allie's scream echoes throughout the stairwell 'til it's abruptly cut off when she collides with the first step. Her body continues to haphazardly tumble with thuds and clangs down the metal stairs, coming to a violent stop on the concrete landing.

I remain frozen with my mouth gaping open in a silent scream.

Allie doesn't make a sound—not a groan or a cry, despite the awkward angle her leg is bent beneath her. Her arms are splayed above her head. Blood slowly seeps out from under her short blond hair, pooling into a crimson halo around her head.

"Allie?" My voice is weak, like I've been screaming this whole time.

She doesn't move.

I take a step, about to go to her, when a hysterical voice turns me around. "What did you do?"

I stare into the frantic wide eyes of the girl from the fire escape, the one Allie hugged.

"Did you ... did you push her?" But it's not really a question. It's an accusation.

I can see the blame in her glassy-eyed stare. But she's not focused on my face; she's looking down ... at my hand clutching Allie's pink wig. I drop it like it's burning my skin. Panic begins to creep over me like crawling vines.

"You did. You pushed her." Her words are thorns, penetrating my flesh.

I take a step back, shaking my head. My lungs constrict, and I can't draw in enough air. This can't be happening. She stares at me like I'm some kind of monster, and I want to shrink into nothing. I take another step backward. She opens her mouth. I shake my head faster, silently begging. I continue to increase the distance between us, moving farther away from her. I need to disappear before she—

A horrific, bloodcurdling scream vibrates throughout my bones.

Doors click open. Two large bodies in black rush by from behind, brushing past me. Several more people enter from the fire escape. Their faces blur. I'm unable to focus. Color and voices move around me. But no one goes to her. Allie's still lying in her blood, needing someone to save her. My heart is beating so fast, I have to press my hand to the wall to stay on my feet.

"What's wrong?" a girl asks, her attention drawn to the screaming girl, yet to notice the broken body at the bottom of the stairs.

But the massive bouncer who first entered sees Allie and his stature changes, taking on an authoritative stance. His voice bellows, "Get them out of here!"

The other body in black forces the small group back onto the fire escape, keeping the devastation hidden behind him. The screaming girl is sobbing now, the only one left in the stairwell ... other than me. But no one seems to notice me, except for her. She grasps the muscular arm of the bouncer closest to her, pointing ... directly at me. But he's too busy locking the door leading to the fire escape.

The bouncer in charge lowers his voice and speaks into the cuff of his shirt, "I need the E team to stairwell five. Now."

Air moves around me as the door behind me is shoved open again. A different guy dressed in black brushes past me.

I slip through the opening just as I hear the lead bouncer shout orders at him, "Lock down all entrance points into this stairwell. Don't let anyone come or—"

And then the door clicks shut, cutting him off.

A tall, thinner, but no less intimidating, male moves in front of the closed door with his hands clasped in front of him.

I turn and take a step into the dark, my senses overwhelmed with the sudden inundation of strobing lights and pounding bass. I stare, unfocused, and release a quivering breath. I can't feel a thing other than the frantic beat of my heart. Bodies dance seductively along the railing, arms floating in the air, hands gripping hips. I remain paralyzed by the twisting vines of panic around my limbs.

Hands grip my shoulders. I blink up into bright blue eyes.

"Lana? Are you okay?" Parker examines my face with concern.

I cannot find the words to respond to his question. Am I okay? No. I am not. I am so far from being okay that I am nothing.

He calls to me again, "Lana?"

I fight to break free from the suffocating restraints holding me mute.

"Parker?" I utter feebly.

None of this feels real. I'm stuck in a slow-moving dream.

"Are you hurt?" he asks when I continue to stand there, staring into his eyes.

He scans my body, searching for injuries. His inspection comes to a sudden halt. Parker wraps his hands around my wrists and holds them up. A spray of blood glistens along the back of my left hand, and pink hairs are entangled around the fingers of my right. I yank free from his grip, my pulse firing rapidly.

Parker reaches into his pocket and hands me a pressed handkerchief. I take it from him and frantically scrub at my hands, smearing red stains on the pristine white cloth.

Raising his right cuff to his mouth, Parker talks into it, "Find my brother. Tell him I need him on the mezzanine. Now."

I inspect my trembling hands, turning them over to make sure I'm rid of all the evidence. Parker eases the cloth from my grip, stuffing it into his pants pocket.

He gently cups my face. "Everything's going to be okay."

I'm lost to my hyperventilating breaths, unable to connect with what he's telling me.

"Lana?" He forces me to focus on him. "I've got this. But you need to leave. Okay?"

The panic is wrapping around me, tighter and tighter.

"Don't say anything to anyone about what happened," Parker instructs.

"But I didn't—" I begin in a rush.

"Don't," he interrupts firmly. "Not a word."

He thinks I did it, that I pushed her—just like the screaming girl in the stairwell.

Parker leans in and presses a kiss to my forehead, murmuring, "I'll take care of everything."

I take a step back, at a loss. He truly believes I'm capable of *that*?

"What's going on?" Joey asks from behind Parker. "Some guy said … "

Parker turns to face his brother.

"Lana?" Joey looks from me to Parker. "Everything okay?"

"No," Parker responds, his spine lengthening with his cursed *Confidence*. "A girl fell down the stairs. The EMTs are taking her to the hospital, but I need you and Lana to leave in case the cops show up." He reaches into his pocket and pulls out a car key. "There's a door on the opposite side, downstairs. Go through it. Take the elevator to the first level. Your Jeep will be there along with your phone. I'll get her friends and meet you"—he hesitates for a moment—"at the golf course. Wait for me."

Parker looks to me again, caressing my cheek, "Say nothing."

Joey takes hold of my hand. "I've got her."

Parker looks down at our clasped hands and scowls.

In the next second, Joey is guiding me along the mezzanine. I look back just as Parker disappears through the black door leading to the stairwell, talking into his cuff.

Joey navigates us down the stairs and around the perimeter of the crowded dance floor. Bodies brush by in a streak of color and jostling of flesh. I can't focus on anything other than the hand holding mine and the blue shirt in front of me.

When we reach the black door concealed in the dark corner, Joey knocks and an unseen hand immediately opens it. It falls closed behind us after we pass through. A tall guy with a blond buzz cut stands behind it silently. He struts over to what looks like a closed garage door and pulls on a strap, revealing a freight elevator. We enter and the door comes crashing down behind us, shutting us off from the booming music and chattering voices.

Within the quiet box, the inner chaos overtakes me—Vic's threats, Allie's fall, the girl's screaming, Parker's warning ... I collapse against the wall, my unfocused eyes trained on the floor. My mind is whirling. My pulse is thrumming. I clench my shaking fists and concentrate on breathing, trying to free myself of panic's strong hold.

"Lana." Joey's voice finds me, firm and soothing.

I lift my head.

Joey has the elevator control in his hand, his eyes steadied on me. He doesn't say anything for a moment, just holds me in his brilliant blue gaze.

"Nothing bad's going to happen to you, I promise." He sounds so certain, like he has the ability to control our fate. "Do you believe me?"

I blink away the tears stinging my eyes and swallow against the lump lodged in my throat. "It's too late."

I cover my eyes with a hand, wanting to hide from the cruel reality. Images too real and graphic to ever forget … Allie sprawled motionless, her blood seeping into the concrete around her. The cold disconnect in Vic's eyes just before he shoved her. And me, standing above Allie with her bright pink wig clenched in my fist, unable to move. Then there's that scream … that high-pitch, horror-movie scream. I swear it's still ringing in my ears.

And I *left* Allie … at the bottom of those stairs. I abandoned her. I should have stayed with her. I don't even know if she was still breathing.

"We need to go back. I need to make sure she's still alive," I plead, strangling a sob.

"The girl? You were there?" His tone is gentle.

I nod. "It was Allie, the girl from the truck. I tried … " My voice breaks as I struggle to speak. "I tried to reach her before he pushed her, but I couldn't."

"Who pushed her?" Joey asks cautiously.

"Vic." His name escapes before I can capture it. I bite my lip to keep from saying more.

I'm not usually this careless. I blame my chemically altered state for allowing the honesty to slip out. This isn't me. I don't overreact like this. I'm the one who holds it together when shit gets bad. But right now, I don't have control over my mind or my body, no matter how hard I fight for it.

Joey's quiet. I watch him carefully, attempting to read the contemplation reflected in his eyes. I try to convince myself that this wasn't a secret I needed to keep. Vic isn't someone I need to protect. But Joey is. And now that he knows the truth, I'm not sure what he'll do with it.

Joey drops the elevator control and slowly walks to me, encircling me in his arms. As soon as he touches me, my breath evens out and the crushing sensation in my chest releases. I squeeze him tight, burying my face in his shoulder, but I don't allow myself to cry. He holds me until the tension in my muscles dissipates and the shaking subsides. His lips press against my temple, and the last tendrils of panic fall away.

I tip my head up.

Joey brushes a strand of hair from my cheek. "There's nothing you can do if we go back. Parker said they were taking her to the hospital. Let's wait and find out if she's okay before we decide what to do, alright?"

I nod, convinced leaving is the best option. He wraps his arms around me one more time, giving me the strength I need to stand on my own before he lets go.

"Ready to get out of here?"

"Yeah," I breathe out, feeling calmer.

Joey pushes the button to lower the elevator, and when he opens it, we step out into a kind of parking lot on the ground floor, presumably for everyone working here. Joey's red Jeep is at the far end, parked in front of the large sliding doors. Holding my hand, he weaves through the maze of cars until we reach it. Joey's cell phone is on the driver's seat. Mine isn't here. I hope Parker will know to bring it with him. I can't afford to lose it.

Two guys in black slide the giant barnlike metal doors open. Joey starts up the Jeep. I half-expect to see red and blue strobes flashing from an ambulance or a police car, but I'm not really surprised when I don't.

Just before Joey pulls forward, a black van flies by the entrance. Joey and I exchange a silent glance, knowing that Allie must be in that van.

Just like the door we entered in the corner of the club, the private garage entrance slides shut behind us as soon as we pull out. We drive through The Point in the dark. Joey doesn't turn on the headlights until we pass the gates and reach the road.

We don't say anything as we drive along the deserted, winding road. I stare out at nothing. The Jeep's top is off and the wind whips loose strands of hair around my head. Joey hands me a sweatshirt when I shiver. I take it from him and slip it on, inhaling the detergent combined with his distinct scent—a mixture of grass and rain.

I lean my forehead against the window, my thoughts continuing to jump around. I close my eyes and inhale deeply. This day should never have happened.

I can sit here and dissect everything I could have done differently from the moment I woke up. But I know everything that's gone wrong tonight is because of Vic.

I clench my jaw so tight, my teeth feel like they might shatter. If I ever see him again, I'm going to *kill* him.

"Why was Vic with you tonight?"

Joey glances at me quickly before looking back to the road. "You don't have to worry. Parker won't bring him to the country club."

"That's not why I'm asking."

Joey shifts uncomfortably. "We're not friends, like I said. We go to the same boarding school. His mother died of cancer a few months ago, and my father asked me to … I don't know, make sure he's okay. My family knows his family. Our fathers went to college together."

"Did you know he was a psychopath?"

"No!" Joey answers adamantly, turning his head to me. "He's not the nicest guy, but I never would've believed he'd push a girl down the stairs. Or that he'd bring a gun. I'm really sorry, Lana, for everything he's done."

"It's not your fault," I reply quietly, sinking into the seat. "His father … is he … powerful?" I have to know what I'm up against since I seem to be the only witness to the truth.

"Vic lives with his grandfather," Joey responds carefully.

When he doesn't say more, I silently urge him to answer the question.

Joey nods regretfully. "He has a lot of connections. He'll cover this up before Vic is accused of anything. That's why I said we should wait to see what happens with Allie before we decide what to do. If it comes down to his word against yours, it won't be good."

I laugh humorlessly. "Of course, because the truth *never* wins." I say this more to myself than to Joey. I turn away from him, the muscles in my jaw knotting up again.

The engine whirring and the tires crunching along the dirt road fill the silence. Staring out the side window, I attempt to focus on our surroundings for the first time since we veered off Sherling's paved roads. I have no idea where we are. It's dark. There aren't any streetlights … or houses. Just woods. The forest appears endless. The tall silhouettes feel like they're closing in around us.

I've never been outside of Sherling before tonight. That town has a way of trapping people within its borders. They're deceived into believing their miserable existence is an inescapable sentence of minimum wage jobs and child support payments.

I can't say I'm convinced there's something better waiting for me outside Sherling, but I refuse to be another one of its stories—predictable and meaningless, doomed to repeat itself. Always the same ending. But, after tonight, I don't think I'll have a say in what happens to me. Maybe I never did.

Parker's words find their way back to me in the quiet. *"Say nothing."*

I know he didn't tell me this to protect me. If Parker really believes I pushed Allie, then he *knows* I'd never admit to it. And Vic isn't the reason either. He didn't even know Vic was with us. And then I remember how he took charge of everything. Insisting Joey leave with me. Confident Allie would be taken to the hospital. Securing our quick exit with just a few words spoken into his cuff.

Parker needs my silence to protect himself.

"Parker's one of the organizers, isn't he?"

Joey hesitates before responding. "You know I can't say anything," he says, concern evident on his face.

But I don't need Joey to confirm it. I know. Parker's always been one to take risks in the name of success. He's cursed with *Confidence*. Failure has never been an option for him. He was our source of amphetamines a couple summers ago when we first started doing everything our parents told us not to. I've heard he's had his hands in other recreational habits as well. He's discreet, so I don't know anything for certain. He's been good at keeping a low profile while being successful at whatever he does. Apparently, he's been busy moving up in the world—fast.

"I won't tell anyone," I promise. "But if the police find out he's one of the people running an illegal club, then … "

"It would be *really* bad for him, especially if someone got seriously hurt," Joey finishes, his meaning understood.

"Right."

A dark pit opens up in the bottom of my stomach. There isn't anything I can do to make this right. The one person who deserves to go down for this is evidently untouchable—and not just because his grandfather would pay to cover it up, but because everyone I remotely care about would suffer, myself included, if I told the truth. I clench my jaw, fighting the urge to scream.

Joey clears his throat, drawing my attention away from all the ways my life sucks right now. "I probably don't want to know this, but how do you know my brother?"

I stop breathing with the question, not sure how honest I should be right now. I'm not about to tell him that Parker was my first kiss. I don't think Parker even knows he was my first kiss. It was two summers ago. I was thirteen, almost fourteen—don't want it to sound *that* bad. Parker and Joey are from Oaklawn, so Parker didn't know anything about me. He thought I was sixteen—not because I told him. He assumed, and I didn't correct him.

Tori and I learned the art of dressing a certain way and applying makeup just right so that we appeared older. I started covering shifts for my mother at Stella's around that time, so I'd also acquired the attitude to back it up. No one's ever questioned my age, even if I can barely see over the bar. It's all in how you present yourself to the world, and I had no fucks to give … until tonight. It helps that I possess an ID that says I'm twenty-two. None of the bars we go to ever blink twice at it. But we live in Sherling. They'd rather have the bodies in the bar and money in their tills.

The first party Tori and I crashed was this high school party at a two-family house a few streets over from Tori's place. Parker was there on "business," just stopping in on his way to a party of his own. But he ended up staying. I may have had something to do with that. He was smooth—still is—saying all the right things and focused on me like I was the only girl in the room. As aloof as I may have tried to act, I was jumping around and screaming with excitement on the inside. Here I was, at my first party, and this absolutely gorgeous guy was hitting on me. I wanted to die!

I did my best to play hard to get. I didn't give him my number when he asked for it. Actually, he *still* doesn't have my number. But when he leaned over in that dark corner I was pressed against, his arm resting on the wall above my head, I didn't move. I didn't push him away. I didn't turn my head. I stood there, perfectly still, and let him press his lips to mine. He teased with slow, playful kisses. And when his tongue entered my mouth, he was slow and gentle. It was... perfect. I think my knees would have given out if the wall hadn't been holding me up.

That was the first and last time Parker Harrison ever kissed me. And it's *the* kiss I will never forget.

Parker must have asked around about me after that because the next time we saw him out, he was pissed. Kissing a thirteen-year-old wasn't exactly good for his reputation, no matter how old he *thought* I was. He had just graduated and wouldn't have been caught dead with a junior, forget about a girl who hadn't even entered high school. Then he saw Nina with us...

Once *they* happened, he was completely off-limits to me. Even when he came around again and got to know me better.

I refuse to give him a chance, no matter how many times he asks.

I must have been quiet too long because Joey suddenly says, "Forget it. Don't tell me."

"It's not like that. We just... see him around," I assure him, trying to sound casual. "He and Nina have a thing. Or whatever. And he sometimes goes to the same bars we do in Sherling."

"You have a fake ID?" Joey asks in surprise.

"You don't?"

Joey shrugs. "I don't really use it. It's one of Parker's old ones. I've never tried to get into bars. The town where I go to school is too small. I'm afraid I'd get busted with it. But I buy beer outside of town sometimes." He shifts uncomfortably again. "So ... he and Nina, not ... " Joey shakes his head. "Never mind."

"Nothing's going on between me and Parker."

"Sorry," he says with a weak smile. "It's happened before ... "

I laugh. "You and your brother have hooked up with the same girl?"

"No," he replies adamantly. "This girl and Parker had a ... *thing*, and when he ended it, she thought I could be the perfect revenge. Except, I couldn't stand to talk to her, let alone kiss her."

"If I remember right, you don't need to talk to kiss," I tease.

I swear his cheeks redden. "You know what I mean."

I've been trying to figure out Joey's curse since the party. But whatever it is, it isn't obvious. As much as he looks like a mussed, youthful version of Parker, he is *nothing* like him. And so ... I guess I should stop comparing them.

"I wouldn't use you as revenge," I tell him sincerely. "I'm not interested in your brother. Most of the time, I wish I didn't know him."

"Me too."

I roll my head against the seat to face him, my cheek pressed against the cool leather, expecting him to be joking. But he just stares out the windshield, his expression a bit solemn. When Joey looks over at me, he offers a half-smile, just enough to give a hint to the dimple on his right cheek.

"This night ... " He lets out a dry laugh before looking back out the windshield with a shake of his head. "I'd say I wish it was over, except ... " He looks at me again, peering right into my eyes. "I keep thinking it'll get better."

"It did. For a couple hours," I say with a weak smile.

The Jeep slows and Joey turns down a dark drive. The headlights shine on a large wooden sign—*Oaklawn Country Club*. We follow a long road that splits the golf course in half, eventually reaching an expansive building with a wall of windows.

A small *Clubhouse* sign is posted in the middle of a dimly lit circular drive where a chandelier glows above carved wooden doors. The building is dark with no signs of movement behind the glass. Joey continues to the left side of the clubhouse where a *Deliveries* sign beckons us into the shadows.

Parking the Jeep on the far side of the dumpster, Joey shuts off the engine. We're not completely concealed here, but at least the Jeep won't be obvious if someone drives by. Unbuckling his seat belt, Joey shifts to face me. He doesn't say anything. We just look at each other, a thousand words confessed within a few seconds of silence.

"You going to be okay?" he asks. The question he's asked so much tonight.

"If I'd known—"

The ringing of his phone keeps the truth from leaping off the tip of my tongue.

Joey looks from me to his beckoning phone, hesitant. He lifts it from the cup holder. "It's Parker," he says apologetically, sliding his thumb across Parker's face to answer it.

Panic rushes in like it never left, quickening my heartbeat, stealing my breath and tying my stomach into intricate knots. I fight the urge to rip the phone out of his hand and demand to know if Allie's okay … if she's alive.

I stare at Joey as he listens, trying to read the expression on his face with each nod. But he won't look at me, and his eyes give nothing away. I'm about ready to scream when he shifts and holds out the phone.

"Parker wants to talk to you."

I stare at it without making a move to take it, suddenly afraid to know the truth. I glance at Joey. His brows rise in encouragement. I smile weakly and accept it, slowly bringing it to my ear.

"Yeah?" My voice is weak.

Music blasts through the speaker. I can hear Tori and Nina singing out of tune at the top of their lungs.

"Hello?" I say louder when no one responds.

"You have nothing to worry about." Parker's distinct voice cuts through the noise.

"What do you mean?" I can feel Joey watching me. "Is she—"

"She's fine, Lana. A broken leg and a concussion. But she'll recover," Parker assures me. "And no one saw you. The guys who found her are contracted not to disclose anything. Keep quiet, and all's good. Nothing's going to happen to you. *I've* got you."

"Okay," I respond quietly, trying to let it all sink in, ignoring the fact that he still thinks I'm the reason she ended up at the bottom of the stairs. And he obviously doesn't know about the screaming girl who thinks the same thing.

"Who are you talking to?" Nina demands impatiently, her voice slurred.

"I'll see you in a bit," Parker says, hanging up before I can ask which hospital she's at.

I slowly lower the phone and hand it back to Joey.

"She's going to be okay." Joey reaches for my hand, enveloping it in his warmth.

Tension immediately seeps from my muscles. Just like that ... I can breathe again, my chest visibly collapsing with the release of air.

"Would Parker lie? Do you think she's really okay?" I ask, knowing how much trouble this could mean for Parker. I've learned to never underestimate what someone is capable of when they're desperate and have everything to lose.

Joey hesitates thoughtfully. "I don't know how he could cover it up. He's done some questionable things to protect himself, but ... he's not a bad guy."

"How can he keep someone from talking?" Regardless of whatever influence Parker has over people, I strongly doubt his weak threats of denied access to a party or social suicide would keep mouths shut.

"I don't think he can," Joey answers simply. "But what can they say other than a girl fell? No one knows, not even the people working there, that he's one of the organizers. And only you and Vic know the truth. They'll have to change locations just in case, but I don't think Parker has anything to worry about. Neither do you."

"Nothing to worry about," I tell myself. Is that true?

Allie's alive. That's a good thing. And she's the only other person who knows what really happened.

## Chapter Nine

*"But he told me he loved me." My mother's words come out muffled with her face buried in the pillow.*

*I stand by the door, peeking in. I'm supposed to be in bed, but my mom's crying woke me up.*

*"And why would you believe him?" my grandmother asks, scowling down at her daughter with her arms crossed. "How many times do I have to tell you, those words are the most poisonous lies ever spewed from a man's mouth?"*

"Want to sit on the green with me while we wait for them?" Joey asks, taking my hand and kissing my palm.

I smile gently. "Sure." I watch him get out of the Jeep. Maybe this day doesn't have to be a *total* nightmare.

Joey meets me at the back of the Jeep. His sweatshirt hangs low on me, creating the illusion that it's the only thing I'm wearing. He fights to hide a grin when he sees me. If he says something stupid like, *I like you in my clothes*, I'm going to throw it at him and get back in the Jeep. Wearing a guy's clothes has this weird effect on them, like it's some twisted sign of ownership. And I'm *not* a possession. Joey offers me his hand instead. I accept it, relieved he keeps whatever comment I saw flash across his face to himself.

We pass between a line of small evergreen trees that separate the delivery area from the golf course and carefully tread down a steep embankment until we're on the finely groomed golf course. Joey leads us to a circular area where the grass is even shorter before letting go of my hand to sit with his legs stretched out in front of him.

I untie my wedges and sink my feet into the lush, cool grass. Sitting down next to him, I pull my knees up to my chest and stretch the sweatshirt over them.

"Are you cold?" Joey asks, wrapping an arm around me and tucking me against his side.

"No, I'm good." I lean into him, resting my head on his chest.

It's so quiet here, it's almost unsettling.

"What colleges are you considering?"

The question seems so out of nowhere. I lean back to look up at him. "What?"

"When we were in the car, Nina said you were going to college. Where are you looking?"

"She was holding a gun to Vic's head, and you remember *that*?" I ask, laughing.

Joey shrugs with a lopsided grin. I laugh again.

"I have no idea why she said that," I tell him. "My guidance counselor keeps sending me home with brochures. But I haven't really thought about it."

"Why not?"

"Why should I? Having a college degree doesn't mean I won't end up working at a coffee shop when I graduate, except I'll have a shitload of student loans to pay off on top of it."

"Don't you have dreams of becoming something ... more?" He studies me intently, waiting. I don't know what makes me more uncomfortable, the question or that he's honestly interested in my answer.

"More than what? College won't change who I am," I say, shifting my focus away from his scrutinizing gaze and leaning back against his side. "I'm not sure what the point is ... wanting more from life than I've already been given. Money doesn't make you happy. I can't see how working eighty hours a week will either."

"Then what will ... make you happy?"

"What's with these questions?" I counter evasively, sitting up straight so that his arm falls away.

"Hey," he soothes, scooting closer and setting his hand on my waist, "I'm just trying to get to know more about you."

"Why?"

"Uh ... because I like you," he offers carefully. "We don't have to talk about you, if you don't want to."

"Let's not."

I know I'm being a bitch and should feel bad, but honestly, I don't trust anyone who wants to know more than my name. And I'm not sure how to explain that to him without making it awkward.

"Would you rather ask me questions? Or ... we can just sit here. They should be here soon."

And now ... it *is* awkward. Crap. Why do I suck at this so much?

I search for something, *anything*, to say so it's not so tense. I've never dated a guy or even been out on a date.

We go to parties and bars where small talk is just that. Stupid, mindless conversation that leads to making out or getting felt up in a dark corner. Even the guy I regularly hook up with keeps the pillow talk to a minimum. It's just about the sex, and that's completely fine with me. I don't *want* anyone to get to know me.

"Tell me something embarrassing," I blurt.

Joey lets out a short laugh. "We can't talk about you, but I have to reveal something embarrassing? That's fair."

"Maybe if you share something vulnerable, I'll feel more comfortable."

I bat my eyes at him dramatically. He chuckles.

"Umm … " He searches the sky in contemplation.

"Don't think too much about it. The first thing that comes to mind."

"The first time I had an erection, I was in church."

"Wha—" I can't even get the word out before I burst out laughing. "Details."

I know that if I could see him clearly his face would be bright red.

He continues, "This really pretty girl was sitting in front of me—I think she went to school with Parker actually—and during the greet-your-neighbor part of the sermon, she turned around, and when she bent over to hug me, I got a face full of boobs. Let's just say, I held on tight until my grandmother swatted me with her purse."

"What'd the girl do?" I ask, still chuckling.

"She laughed, especially when she saw the tent in my khakis. My grandmother was mortified, and my mother yelled, 'William!' so loud that half the church turned around and stared at me cupping my crotch. I had no idea what was happening or how to make it go away. It was undeniably the most embarrassing moment of my life."

My stomach's hurting I'm laughing so hard "That's amazing!" I finally catch my breath. "Why'd she call you William?"

"My full name is three first names, and everyone calls me something different. It even confuses me sometimes."

"Joseph William Harrison?"

He nods slowly. "That's it."

I raise my eyebrows. "Add some Roman numerals to the end and you could be royalty."

Joey laughs. "I'm the furthest thing from honorable."

"Really?" I question, leaning in until we're a breath apart. "I don't know if I believe that," I say, tempting him with a salacious grin.

I watch his mouth part. His eyes don't leave mine. He wraps a hand around the back of my neck and pulls me to him.

I close my eyes, anticipating the touch of his lips. And when they finally find me, my whole world stills. A lightness overtakes me, swirling in my head. His mouth caresses mine, stealing my breath. A small moan escapes at the caress of his tongue. I can't breathe, but I don't want to. I grip the front of his shirt, needing to get closer. Needing him. His arm tightens around my waist. I am lost in him, in this kiss.

Joey slowly pulls away, our breaths mingling in quick pants. His hand still cups my neck as he gently presses his forehead to mine. "I can't tell you how long I've wanted to do that."

Before we can connect again, his phone chimes.

With an apologetic groan, he leans away and pulls it out of his pocket. He reads the screen, then looks across the golf course to the far side of the clubhouse. "They're here. Told us to meet them at the pool."

Four silhouettes approach the waist-high fence surrounding the pool and climb over. I only have a second to process what they're planning before I see someone, who I assume to be Nina, pull her dress over her head.

I turn back to Joey. "Not yet. Okay?"

He grins and nods before texting a reply and setting the phone beside him on the grass.

Without hesitating, he pulls me onto his lap and I straddle him, our lips crashing together. We are not gentle—groping, groaning and grinding. Our breathing is as frantic as our heartbeats. My fingers tangle in his hair. His hands slide under the sweatshirt and grip my bare back. I don't pull away to breathe. I could seriously die kissing him.

Joey pulls the sweatshirt roughly over my head and flips me so I'm lying on top of it, his body pressed to me. His mouth tastes down the lines of my neck and into the revealing slope of the halter. I wrap my legs around him and tilt my head back, consumed by his touch. I tug at the edges of his shirt, desperate to run my hands along his skin. He separates long enough to yank it over his head and toss it on the grass.

His body crushes me in the best possible way and I gasp.

"You feel so good," he murmurs against my neck, sucking the skin below my ear.

I grip him tighter, moving beneath him.

He groans with a heavy breath. "Oh god, Lana, I love you."

I freeze.

Joey begins to lift my shirt, and I grab his hands, stopping him.

"Get off me."

He looks down at me, confusion surfacing beneath the lust. "What?"

I shove hard at his chest. "Get off me!"

Joey rolls to the side, not resisting. Realization and shock flash across his face. His mouth drops open, but nothing comes out. I stand, adjusting my shirt and snatching my shoes.

"Lana!" Joey calls to me, his tone laden with panic. "Don't go."

But I'm already storming away, rage pulsing through my veins. I can feel the muscles along my neck protruding.

"Lana!"

I focus on the pool, blocking him out. He'd better stay the fuck away from me. If he follows me or tries to touch me, I swear I will castrate him.

"Hey!"

My footsteps stumble. The voice is deeper, not Joey's. I turn and am blinded by a bright spotlight.

"Stay right there."

I don't have to see to know he's a police officer. So … I run.

"Stop!"

The pool seems so fricken far away right now. And when I'm halfway there, I watch Parker, Lincoln, Tori and Nina scramble up and out of the pool. They grab their clothes as they run for the fence. The spotlight veers away from me for just a moment to illuminate them. It gives me the second I need to push into the hedges along the side of the clubhouse.

I hear the police car pull out of the delivery area. I consider running for it, but by this time, the four of them are already disappearing into the trees. I can't see what's on the other side, but I have to assume it's where Parker left his car.

As much as I don't want to, I look back to where I left Joey, but I don't see him. A second later, I hear the Jeep start up and pull away. Where's he going?

I'm about to step out of the hedges, not sure where to go, when the police car comes into view again at the pool side of the clubhouse, its spotlight shining on the blue water. I shove back into the hedges, scraping my arms against the prickly branches, just as the light swings up, sweeping along the golf course toward where Joey and I were on the green.

I hug my knees to my chest, trying to make myself as small as possible when the light passes in front of the hedges. I close my eyes, afraid to even breathe. When I open them again, the light is gone and I exhale. I wait for what feels like an eternity before poking my head out. The police car is pulling away, its spotlight still searching the area as it turns onto a road on the other side of the trees. It doesn't stop. Parker must have driven off, which means … they left me.

I stay in the hedges another couple minutes in case the cops decide to circle back. This is pathetic. They really have nothing better to do than to chase after skinny-dippers on a Friday night? Considering we're in Oaklawn, that's probably a major offense.

When I finally emerge from the confines of the hedges, my legs and arms are streaked with fine red scratches, and I'm covered in green needles. Pulling the elastic free, I shake out my hair, tiny green slivers raining down. When I secure it back on top of my head, I realize my headband's missing.

"Shit," I grumble.

That's one of the few nice things I own—an heirloom from my mother that my grandmother gave to her. I try to retrace my steps, searching for it, but it's too dark to see anything in the grass. Giving up, I decide to walk back toward the pool, just in case Joey is parked somewhere near the delivery area or comes back there to get me. I'd rather walk back to Sherling than get in the car with him.

"I love you?" I growl, the words inciting a rush of riotous fury. "What the fuck?"

I can't believe he said that. *Those* words. The worst of all lies.

I clench my fists with my shoes dangling between my fingers. "I love you?!" My stomach rolls and bile rises in the back of my throat.

I can't believe I let him touch me. That I thought for a second that he was actually a decent guy. So stupid!

When I reach the road on the other side of the trees, it's deserted. The street is lined with huge houses with lanterns lit on either side of their doors and at the end of their driveways. The front lawns and hedges are perfectly trimmed, just like the golf course, but no one's on the street. I walk in the direction of the road leading to the main street. The entire time, I'm hexing Joey and every other guy who has ever used those words to seduce or manipulate a girl.

I'm halfway down the road that divides the golf course when headlights flood the dark. I am completely exposed with nowhere to hide. But right now, I don't care if I'm picked up by the police. My feet hurt. I'm cold. And the anger has drained all the life out of me. This night honestly can't get any worse.

The car slows as it nears. It's a gold or tan-colored Land Rover. I keep my head down and continue walking past it when it stops across from me and the driver's window rolls down.

"Lana."

I pause and lift my head.

"Get in."

I stare at Parker for a second before crossing the street toward him, my shoulders slumped in defeat. I open the back door, expecting to find the car full, but it's empty.

"Sit in the front," he instructs.

I close the back door and climb into the passenger seat. "Where is everyone?"

"With Joey. I met him on the side of the road. He said you were still here." Parker comes to a stop at the intersection with the main road and looks at me. "He said it'd be better if I came to get you. The girls were starving, so they went with him. They said to meet them at Stella's."

"If he's going to be there, then just take me home," I tell Parker.

Parker pulls onto the main street, his car still the only one on the road. "What happened?"

I stare at the same encroaching dark forest as before, unable to look at him. "I don't want to talk about it."

"He didn't hurt you, right?" Parker says this like even the idea of it is impossible.

"No," I huff. "He's a liar. Just like everyone else."

Parker doesn't respond. Neither of us speaks as he drives through Oaklawn, eventually crossing into Sherling.

"You don't lie."

I turn my head, his words cutting through the prolonged silence. "How do you know?"

"I remember you telling me once that you don't lie—ever. And ... I believe you. You've never lied to me, even when I wished you had." He releases a low chuckle. "You really don't, do you?"

"No, I don't," I reply simply.

"Then can I ask you one question that you promise to answer?"

I shift in my seat so I'm angled toward him, intrigued by the request. This could be dangerous. But Parker doesn't exactly seem like the kind of guy who wants to explore the depths of my soul. If Joey had asked this, my answer would have been an automatic no. I narrow my eyes, considering Parker's motive.

He grins when I hesitate. "It's just one question, Lana. How bad could the truth be?"

I lean back against the seat. "If I agree, what do I get in return?"

Parker laughs. "What do you want?"

"Stop hooking up with Nina," I tell him without thinking. And I'm not sure *why* this is my demand. I don't want him, and I'm not jealous of them. But it's something that's always bothered me. Perhaps because I know how toxic they are together, and I want better for Nina. And maybe for Parker too.

"Done," he answers immediately. "I'd actually already decided that earlier tonight, so your wish was kind of a waste. So that means I get to ask you anything, and you have to tell me the truth."

I exhale in resignation. "What do you want to know?"

Parker flashes me a wily grin. "I didn't say I was going to ask you now. I think I'll save it."

I roll my eyes. "You're so dramatic."

Parker laughs. "Always."

The streetlights of Sherling fill the darkness. Cars and buses pass on either side of us. Exhausted, I half-focus on the closed storefronts hidden by graffiti-tagged gates and the people loitering outside of the few bars that are still open.

Parker pulls into Stella's pocked dirt parking lot. I scan the cars in search of Joey's Jeep.

"He's not here," Parker assures me. "I texted him to go."

"Thanks," I say softly, unclicking the seat belt. "Well, I'd say it was fun, but it wasn't."

Parker gives me a sympathetic smile. "I was serious earlier when I said I got you, Lana. I do. Anytime you need me, I'm here." He opens up his console and pulls out my phone. "You have my number now. Use it anytime."

"You hacked into my phone?" I narrow my eyes. He smiles wickedly. "You're trouble."

Parker smiles wider, not denying it. I realize a second too late that I'm staring at him, lost in his seductive smile. His hand brushes against my cheek, tucking loose strands of hair behind my ear. I pull away when his thumb caresses my lower lip.

He grins. "We will happen, you know."

I release an exasperated sigh. "Really, Parker?"

I shove open the passenger door with an annoyed grunt and slam it behind me. It's not until my bare feet make contact with the rocky ground that I remember my shoes are in his car. But he's already pulling away. I hold my hand up to stop him just as a truck pulls out and blocks me from view.

I tap on my screen to call him; it's dead. "Of course."

I delicately navigate the terrain on the balls of my feet, grimacing in pain with each stone-ridden step. I squeeze past the drunks waiting in line to get in and pop out on the other side with a heavy breath.

Tori and Nina are easy to find halfway down in a booth, giggling uncontrollably. Nina has her wet hair braided to the side while Tori's is pulled back in a knot at the nape of her neck. They look like they've had the best night. Their table is littered with a half-dozen plates of pie slices in various stages of consumption and a large red plastic cup of Coke in front of each of them. I consider leaving, not wanting to ruin it.

Tori stops laughing when I come to a stop next to their table.

"Lana! Holy shit, where the fuck have you been?" she exclaims, jumping out of the booth and wrapping me in a quick, tight embrace.

I hug her back, inhaling the sharp chlorine scent on her skin.

She steps back and scans me. "You look … horrible!"

I blink.

"Omigod," Nina gasps. "What happened to you? Did you get in a fight?"

I stare at her, confused. She's staring at my chest.

I look down, unable to see what she's focused on. But I do see the angry red scratches marring my arms and legs. "What?"

"You have a bruise," she says, gently touching my collarbone. It's tender but not bad. It must be from when Vic pinned me against the wall. "Seriously, what happened to you?"

"Can we sit?" I ask, so tired, I feel like I might fall over.

The girls slide back into the booth, and I slip in next to Tori, slumping down against the cracked vinyl.

"So?" Tori demands when I don't start talking right away.

I open my mouth, but nothing comes out. I have no idea where to even start.

"What happened with Joey?" Nina blurts.

I close my eyes and groan between clenched teeth. "I never want to see another Harrison ever again. Not a single one of them. Ever."

"He didn't do that to you, did he?" Tori asks, ready to be just as pissed off as I am.

"No. This is courtesy of Vic." I focus on Nina. "Did you give him back his gun?"

"What?!" Nina replies, shocked. "No way. It's right … " She shuffles through her satchel. Her eyes narrow in confusion as she starts dumping items on the table. "I swear it was in here." She looks up, at a loss. "I have no idea where it is."

"He has it," I tell them. "Stupid fuck. Did you see him when you left?"

They both shake their heads.

"What did he do to you?" Tori asks.

I grind my teeth together, knotting the muscles in my jaw. With a shake of my head, I rake a hand through my loose bangs.

"Lana," Nina implores, "you have to tell us. You know we'll protect you no matter what."

"Let me think about it," I tell them, needing to figure out what could potentially happen if they knew.

I don't want to risk them being involved if it goes to shit. I have no idea if Allie really is okay. Or if that screaming girl told anyone what she saw. Hell, Vic could claim to be a witness to me pushing her, and I have no way of proving that I didn't. Telling Nina and Tori could put them at risk. I don't trust Vic not to go after them, especially if he thinks they may be a threat.

"Can we go home?" I ask with a heavy sigh. "Every inch of me either hurts or is covered with dirt."

"Lana, where are your shoes?" Nina exclaims with a laugh.

"In Parker's car. I took them off when I started walking back from the country club."

"You really are having the worst night ever," Tori declares.

"You have no idea."

## Chapter Ten

*"She isn't your curse." I keep my eyes shut at the sound of my grandmother's voice. "You can love her."*

*"I'm trying," my mother whispers. "But every time I look at her, I see the truth, and I know I've lost him."*

*"Not because of her," my grandmother says gruffly.*

*"Yes," my mother counters sadly, "because of her."*

"Here," Nina says, holding out a pair of sparkly black flip-flops.

"You have flip-flops in your purse?" I ask incredulously.

"You try wearing stilettos for hours. Of course I carry around a pair of flip-flops. They've saved me more times than I can count, and now, they're saving you. So, you're welcome."

"Thank you," I say, apology in my tone. I slide my feet into them and am grateful for the gargantuan purse Nina lugs around with her everywhere.

We step out of Stella's and start walking across the parking lot.

"My place?" I confirm.

The girls nod, knowing I'm within walking distance. The walk isn't nearly as shady as a bus ride at two o'clock in the morning.

Tori hands me my leather jacket, and I happily put it on. "Thanks."

"Parker says we're done," Nina announces.

I try to read the emotion behind the declaration but can't. At least *Parker* told me the truth.

"Are you okay with this?" I ask delicately.

She shrugs indifferently. "You know he doesn't mean it. But whatever. He's kind of a slut, and he definitely doesn't respect me. So he can go to hell."

I laugh.

"What did Joey do?" Tori asks. "He a slut too?"

"I don't know," I tell them, "but he *is* a liar."

Tori sighs, shaking her head. "So no more Harrisons." She pauses and bites her lip. "Except ... I'm going out with Lincoln again ... so you may have to tolerate Joey. But I'll try to make sure it's from a distance."

I study her curiously. "You're serious about Lincoln? You really like him?"

A girlish smile emerges. "He's *so* nice. And his body? Un-be-lievable."

"At least one of us ended up with a good one," Nina says. We round the corner and start down my street. "I think we need to visit the 'party in a bag.' I remember seeing a joint in there, and we could definitely use it."

"Definitely," I agree adamantly, searching my pockets. I pull out the switchblade, wishing I'd had it earlier in the stairwell with Vic. And then I pat the inside pocket and reach for the small plastic bag. Before I can put the switchblade back in my pocket, a car pulls up beside us.

"Lana Peri?" a deep booming voice confirms.

Instinctively, Nina rolls her hand beneath mine, removing the knife from it and slipping it in her purse. A beam of light blinds me just as I drop the bag of drugs to the ground and step on them.

"What was that?" a female voice asks. A car door shuts.

I raise my hands in the air to show that they're empty, familiar with the routine.

"Are you Lana Peri?" the guy asks again.

"Yes," I tell him, shielding my eyes from the flashlight.

"Take a step this way."

With a sigh, I do.

The female officer snaps a pair of rubber gloves over her hands and picks up the plastic bag. "Looks like you've been having an eventful night, Lana."

"Step behind the vehicle," the male officer instructs.

"Are you ladies with her?" the female asks Nina and Tori.

I silently connect with them, and they know what I want them to do.

"We just got here," Nina tells them.

"What are your names?" she asks, setting the drugs on the trunk and pulling out paper and a pen to write them down.

I don't hear what else they say because the male officer's voice is too loud in my ear.

"Place your hands on the trunk. We're arresting you for possession of narcotics. Do you understand?"

I nod.

The female officer comes around behind me while the male officer drops the drugs into an evidence bag. "Do you have anything sharp on your body before I pat you down?"

"No," I answer flatly, staring at the back window, shutting every emotion down.

My face doesn't flinch with the slightest expression. I don't move when her hands pat down my body, tucking her fingers along my waistline. This part is never fun. She grips my wrist and brings it behind my back.

The weight of the cool metal settles around my wrists as the handcuffs click, tightening. I turn my head away from the flashing lights as the male officer grips my arm, moving me toward the open door of the police car.

Tori stands next to Nina, biting her lip. Nina has her arms crossed, wearing a defiant scowl. I want to assure them that I've got this. That everything's going to be okay. But I don't know if that's true. I have no idea what I'm being brought in for, other than possession. There could be so many reasons they were looking for me—theft, assault, armed robbery, trespassing or, depending on who's been talking, attempted murder.

The officer places his hand on the top of my head as I duck down. And that's when I see the red Jeep pull up in front of the house next to us. A phone to his ear, he stands up on his seat so I can see him.

He mouths the words, *Keep your mouth shut.*

Not a problem. I don't plan on confessing to anything. Even if I did do it.

I watch Nina and Tori disappear in the distance with Lincoln and Joey by their sides, staring after the police car. Usually they'd be asked a lot more questions. Thankfully, the cops are only interested in me and chose not to call backup to bring the girls in too. I don't dwell on it, although their rush to take me in should concern me.

The ride to the station is uneventful. As is the booking process.

I don't know how long I've been in the holding cell, shivering on the slab that's meant to be a bed, when a balding male cop finally unlocks the door.

"The detectives have some questions for you," he tells me.

He takes hold of my arm and escorts me to a small interrogation room with gloomy gray walls. I sit in a hard metal chair at a dented wooden table and glance up at the two-way mirror in front of me.

Things just got serious. This has nothing to do with possession.

I take a breath, trying to steady my pulse. But it continues to pick up speed.

A few minutes later, the door opens and two men in suits walk in, nodding toward the cop, who leaves us. They say something, probably their names, but I'm not listening. I'm staring at the small figure behind them, clutching a rose-colored duster sweater around her body.

I stand up in a sudden movement, the chair scraping against the floor. "What is she doing here?"

"Lana," my mother says gently, "it's okay. They said I needed to be here."

A lanky, bald detective points to a chair in the corner of the room, near the door. She smiles at him nervously and sits.

"Have a seat," the detective with the horrible complexion and bushy mustache instructs firmly.

Keeping my eyes on my mother, I lower myself onto the chair again. She's ghostly pale, and her eyes are rimmed red. I know she's not well, and she shouldn't have to be here.

The detective with the mustache—Freddy, I'll call him since I missed his name and his skin reminds me of a nightmare—sits across from me with a file in his hand. He proceeds to recite my Miranda rights and has me sign the paper stating I understand them. The other detective leans against the wall next to the door with his arms folded.

"Want to let you know that we're recording this right now," he tells me, tilting his head toward the two-way mirror. A red light is faintly visible on the other side.

I flip it off with an obnoxious smile.

"Nice," he mutters.

I give him a let's-get-on-with-this look of impatience as I lean back in the chair with my arms crossed. If they actually did their homework and looked me up, they know they're about to waste a lot of time because I don't talk. Ever. No matter how long they keep me in this depressing room.

I watch him flip open the file folder on the table between us, and he spreads a couple grainy photos in front of me. Now I know why I'm here. It's next to impossible to make out the faces, the imagery is so poor, but my blinding blond hair is hard to miss, as is the gun in the hand of the guy dressed in black.

"What have you been up to tonight, Lana?"

I raise my eyes to look at him, my face expressionless. And that's how I remain for the next hour or two. It's hard to tell since there isn't a clock in this oppressive room. They ask questions. I don't answer.

"Tell us who the male with the gun is, Lana. Make it easier on yourself," the detective with the pockmarks along his jawline asks me for the hundredth time. "If you didn't do anything wrong, then you have nothing to worry about."

The corner of my mouth quirks. His eyes narrow into a glower. I know better. The truth won't save me. There's a reason *Honesty*'s my curse.

My mother continues to look frailer with each passing second. I don't want her in here, but I'm a minor, and they don't want to worry about my rights being violated if they question me without a parent present. It's worse for her than it is for me. And I'm concerned she's about to pass out.

"Could you get my mother some water?" I ask the detective who's remained standing by the door with his arms crossed. I think he's supposed to look intimidating. It's not working.

The detective glances at my stricken mother and back to Freddy.

Freddy gives him a subtle nod and glances at the two-way glass, making sure the red light is on and the camera's still recording this pathetic interview.

"Lana, we have you on tape at the convenience store. We have the statement from the clerk. We recovered the stolen lottery tickets from your possession. You know who the guy is holding the gun. All you have to do is tell us; otherwise, it looks like you're his accomplice. Either way, you're obstructing the investigation."

I glance at my mother again. She wipes a tear from her cheek with a shaky hand. I try to reassure her with a small smile. She bites her lip to keep from crying.

"Does she really need to be in here?" I ask again for the tenth time.

The door opens. The wall art reappears with a bottle of water. Once he's through the door, I notice someone's behind him. A tall, regal-looking man in a suit. His salt-and-pepper hair is slicked back—not in a slimy mob-boss way, but in a distinguished I-have-money-and-power kind of way. His vibrant blue eyes take in the room with an assessing glance, from my mother to Freddy, and then steady on me. His face is expressionless, but his eyes tell me everything I need to know. He's confident, intelligent, and he gets exactly what he wants ... just like his son.

"This interview is over," he announces.

My mother stands, her crystal-blue eyes wide. "Niall?"

The man's face softens when he turns toward her, a small, sad smile on his face. "Faye," he acknowledges solemnly, like he's silently apologizing for something.

Her eyes flood with tears that she blinks back, gratitude and relief dancing in them. The relief confuses me—like she knows he *will* fix this.

"Don't worry. I'll take care of her. Why don't you wait out in the hall for me?"

My mother nods, quickly glancing at me before slipping out of the room. With the click of the door closing, Niall focuses back on us—or I should say, on me. He stares at me stoically, his face not giving anything away.

Freddy's jaw clenches. "Niall, *you're* her lawyer? I didn't think you took these kind of cases."

Niall Harrison doesn't respond to his question. "I need a moment alone with my client."

This isn't over…

THE *Cursed* SERIES - PART 2

REBECCA DONOVAN

# Acknowledgments

This story was determined to be written, even after years of writing and re-writing the first four chapters. I learned a lot during those years—mostly, that I needed to be kind to myself, even when I felt like I was failing. *Especially* when I felt like I was failing.

I am surrounded by beautiful and strong women who encouraged and supported me during the time I felt most fragile. When I questioned who I was and what I was doing. They never faltered. And I am so very grateful to have them in my life. Thank you for not giving up on me!

And thank you to you, my readers, who have waited patiently for the words to find me again. They have. And, oh, do they have a story to tell you!

This is just the beginning …

## About the Author

Rebecca Donovan, the *USA Today* and *Wall Street Journal* bestselling YA author of **The Breathing Series** and **What If**, lives in a small town in Massachusetts with her son. Influenced and obsessed with music, Rebecca can often be found jumping around at concerts, or on a plane to go see one. She's determined to *experience* (not just live) life. And then write about it.